Published by
*f*eatherproo*f* **books**
Chicago, IL
www.*f*eatherproo*f*.com

First edition
∞

Library of Congress Cataloging-in-Publication data is available for this title.
ISBN 13: 978-1-943888-29-0

Edited by Jason Sommer
Cover design by Zach Dodson
Title page design by Soren
Interior design by Jason Sommer
Proofread by Alan Heathcock

Set in Baskerville

Printed on demand

FAILURE TO COMPLY

a novel by Cavar

*fe*atherpr*oof* BOOKS

Chicago, IL

FAILURE
to COMPLY

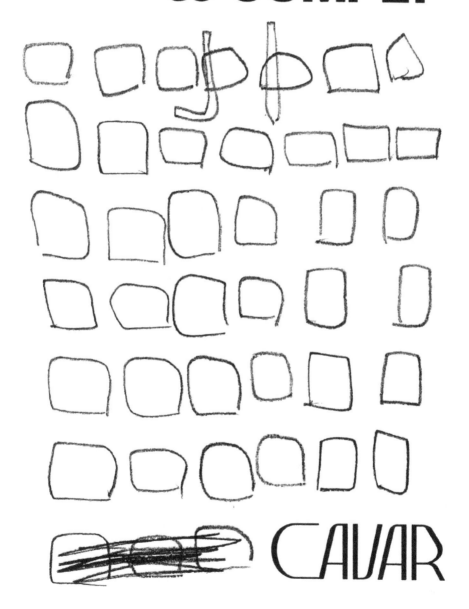

CAVAR

for my kin

to[ward] a way out

Table of Contents

Prelude

the long necked axe struck clean out of me my most beloved memories. Had my beloved been here with me, they could not have helped. There are things, I learn, that they cannot do. As for me, there was never hope for correction, as all my impurities have long known love.   T h e r e comes a time when the bad is loved so much it can neither be corrected nor lived without. Love is like a binding seal, a wax to keep the imperfection in, thick enough for water to skim yet never penetrate. Without the love, we become easy to replace.

What is to be replaced when the eyes are shut. When the eyes are on
        other things

An axe turned me from a loved into a a silence. This was final cut, the thing to separate me from all I loved. Here I was at the brink of every-thing

real. Nothingness wrung cool and sure in its wake, but I would not know, because by then I was long gone.

Slated for replacement, I was naked: an Uncitizen. Eventually I would receive a gown, light as air, translucent and white, all white, so white it hurt my eyes even when the lids were shut. The opacity of a Citizen's clothes turned when I wore them to a jokelike gauze, transparent as

but I ahead myself. Know I was wrapped in a gauze that served
no purpose but shame.

With the swing of an axe, one makes a Citizens' arrest.

a process by which the one swinging reasserted hisorher status as Citizen by stripping an Impure body of
its own

And what does that make me? I was a person

soon ago. Then RSCH saw me hide, brought me back into the fold to be cast out once more. I am trying to be clear with you but I can only speak in riddles. I've lost all the meaning that lived in my memories. I don't know which tense I'm living in. But this is not the future. I've lost the words to say what I have to say. I used to have a name. I used to have a place. I have a face I shouldn't see. I have a body I shouldn't hold   the way I do.

I know this. In life, there are the directives. there are those who obey, those who are obeyed, and the non-existent in between. there is no love, I learned; there is only power. Love is a means of pushing power down easy, of opening the throat. It is said

> i do this because i love you.
> why do you do this there
> are people who love you.

So it is said:
> love becomes   the direction and force and frequency of pow-
> er. transmuted. one body to the next. Love is the soft touch of
> power. Love is the RSCH to its Citizen, love is the perverse,
> love is the you're sick please better for me sickbetter for all of
> us sickandgetbetter let us be whole and love again—let love be
> the blade.

And it is said I am   a person been held captive for all these long years, for none of which she had a clock. She is i. She is me. She is in a holding cell. She is somewhere else. She could not mark the time. She has no proof. She has no body to speak of and no-place. So she is many at once.

And lacuna requisites the whole

The beverage was blue, glowing quiet power. Microchips failed in the face of whatever was inside. Magnets dulled. Minds cracked. Metal turned to hot pain and only flesh and blood and bone were spared. It was an addition of dead-weight. Dragged, dragged, drugged down. Immobilized as a means of torture and correction, and also of detection. When a subject who passed outwardly as Pure was brought in for questioning, they were first measured all over to determine their adjacency to the correct size, which changed each year. Their blood was cross-referenced with their birth data. The constant backlog of subjects for assessment produced yearly chaos at the containment centers as RSCH determined who was to be let go, who was to stay, and who was to be let go but chipped

(chipping by a RSCH was not chipping, definitionally speaking, because chipping was a violent crime against the once-Pure body and RSCH was invested in the maintenance of purity.

(so it was instead called maintenance)

because they would likely need to be contained once more in a coming year. In the year whose end RSCH alone declared with pageantry, and all whose ages did not increase and whose lives did not progress were the first of that coming year to be gone, to be axed away into elsewhere.

(do you understand   the words
                         belong to them)

1. RSCH is hiring again.

They haven't hired like this since before I was born, taking only trainees schooled in Truth from birth. Yet the notification blinked on every HoloScreen in the Community, jarring bytes of color and sound. With the re-issue of their internal guidelines for public health, I knew, RSCH had detected an increase in cases of deviance; I suspected their search was for drs to attend to the veritable epidemic in our midst.

And so RSCH advertised RSCH, this thing of and beyond Citizenship, stretching all imposing over it, to the everyday Citizens, scrolling with their pupils through the notifications in their AR contacts. They strode uniform over barren sidewalks flanked by NewGrass eyes darting to one side and another. I felt sad, almost, before remembering that any of them would have me obliterated if given the chance. They'd get rid of me, claiming I had never been alive at all. The NewGrass breezed beside Citizens' feet. Each body took an upright stride, straight-backed and intentional, as the healthy body should.

From where I sat, the face of the Community was barren, abandoned for the AR. There was little to watch with unaugmented eyes but the bodies and their calculated movements. With the widespread acceptance of HoloScreens and its accompanying AR contacts, the background world has fallen into misuse and all gone monochrome. From my space among the trees I saw a world of wide NewGrass expanses and a dense, translucent whiteness: white houses, white garments, people who aspire to look like window-glass. Whose skin, despite transparent aspirations, came most frequently in various opaque shades of brown and beige, which were rendered irrelevant by the contacts, which displayed in their stead only a word, another measure, which was of the utmost importance because it was True.

Words not so much in separation but in a practice of strained and particularized togetherness. We were differently hued, but this was oldworld talk which should not be thought. Yet always, RSCH was Light.

Bodies, too, though shrouded in loose white linens, were marked by sex. RSCH **is hiring**, maker of the contacts, was guardian of Truth.

As a child I watched my peers study their numbers. Back then, I had the contacts, too, and studied my own with attention: height, weight, blood pressure, heart rate. Because we could not touch each others' skin—an act of perversity worth a diagnosis of Acute Self-Sovereignty Dysfunction, or ASSD1—this is the way we became of each other. **RSCH is hiring**, calling upon others to help protect us from ourselves, from the bodies we are bound to   mismanage.

RSCH is hiring. We saw the message uncontacted because it was projected against the sky, the lid. Some other Uncitizen, augmented by one form of illicit tech or another, must have found away to siphon the message from the Network and reproduce it by themself. I looked to Reya at my far left and asked them with my eyes if they could also see the counterfeit above us. From the distance I could see them, a basket of fungi on one sweating arm, sharp dotted chin upturned.

Reya did not watch the ad but instead the sun in its timed daily rise, leaning forward on their shining silver crutches. When the timed breeze came, Reya's black unwieldy hair, thick and waist-length, rose and fluttered with the leaves on the trees, which themselves swayed and bowed slightly in the wind. Feeling my eyes on them, they turned, beginning to make their way back to my side. With their free hand they reached out to touch me, brushing pearls of dirt from my thinning chest hair. Last night, we slept in a tiny ditch, beneath the moss and dirt with holes poked for breathing. This morning we ate dirty leaves and sweet roots from our newly-excavated hole. I returned their hand to them, guiding it to their hair, brushing until stray detritus hit the ground by the base of their crutches.

RSCH is hiring. The text began to move closer to our hiding place, drifting through the sky. I heard a rustling far away and saw a four-legged silhouette in the distance. Something was attached to its back. It was a small, noticeable protrusion that seemed to wave as the Uncitizen moved, the message bobbing with it from the sky. Another rustle. I dug my filthy fin-

---

1 ASSD had two primary subtypes, one concerned with inaccurate self-image and one concerned with a defect in social comportment. The name doesn't matter much, just as mine does not. It's all about the thing the name is used to speak.

gernails into my palms. The silhouette and the rustle grew closer, the pirate message glitching in the now-risen sun. Reya and I dove into our sleeping hole, recovering with dirt and moss, disappearing at the still-nearing sounds.

RSCH is hiring. As a result of an exponential rise in Uncitizens terrorizing the Community, we call upon the Pure to uphold Truth and Order.

RSCH is

Do you w

the futu

good na

hiring.

ant to be

re of our

tion?

Call me a projection. I am
writing this for public record.

RSCH is hiring. Do you want to make the future of our good nation?

RSCHishiring. Will you work for Truth? Will you lie in falsehood? Would you like to work for us for all of us?

RSCHishiring RSCHishiring.

RSCH sees your interest   RSCH is excited to take you in

I heard the axe come down on the four-legged thing and its wail, its head-splitting wail, penetrated the earth. When we finally emerged, the message laid long-fallen.

Everything is on the rise, everything is now and everything is serious. The news is no longer in the sky. I think I've swallowed something I shouldn't. I hope it makes it to my second stomach of its own accord, or else I'll have to fish around and put it there, before I can reject whatever sharpness I had to swallow for lack of another option.

I crouch behind an overturned log, peering up toward where the notification used to be. Its echo hangs above, imposing. I shield my face as if the message itself has eyes.

keep nothing / in a diary
you'd have pause
to share among enemies; informants / ears
and eyes of the universe

I used to live in a house, two-floored and white and surrounded by green green NewGrass, just like every other in the long line of houses running greater still as far as I could see. Each sat three feet from the start of the sidewalks flanking monorail lanes, the use of which was earned through satisfactory job performance only. We got in and out using our contacted eyes, each identifiable by RSCH within their massive sprawling database, invisible to the naked untrained eye but nevertheless Truthful, Real, Real as RSCH   made it.

Each day I left my house to walk to school (no students could use the monorails as we did not work. We took the sidewalk path, pace-tracked by the contacts. Each morning we got our vital signs checked, and again each evening when we were to return home. I attended school until I renounced my personhood, just as all the other students, watching the far off distant forest in which I now live as if it were made of violence.

Every adult works with data. I don't know a single Citizen who doesn't. Of course, there is RSCH, but they are not   they   are   Citizens, but strictly speaking, they're

I mean, each adult Citizen goes to work as we go to school, the better

> *Better* is the RSCH word used to evaluate efficiency and precision. We are rewarded as Citizens for self-betterment as Citizens.
>
> Self-betterment betters the writ large.

ones on monorails and the worse on sidewalks. The more efficiently you sort data, the more credit you make, the more status symbols you might obtain, not only monorail use but also the use of things like AR contact applications or themes for your Network page. These are all crucial parts of navigating the social milieu.

What was the data? We were. It, us. We saw none of the substance of the data we were, but shuffled it around in codes written in an english only RSCH knew. This was the top layer. It looked like our english, but came in sentences lacking meaning, covering the vital signs that lay below.

This different english did not have a name; it did not have its own special lines and shapes, it was not like all the forms of babble they had out there, before. In school we understood the babble   was af front to Truth, translation muddying Fact. These were the dark times when the night could swallow a body and there was no RSCH to enlighten up and down the streets within our heads. There were no contacts, no context, no alleviating ourselves the unknown.

Though we remain unable to work with the raw data, we know it to be Truth because it is RSCH. The truth comes in sets of sentences like this:

> "Here is the girl.
> The girl has a horse.
> The girl went shopping for juice and bread.
> The girl went home and saw her mother."

The sentences are designed to be dropped into file folders marked by keyword. One would know to distribute pieces of this file to the folder labeled "the girl" and the subfolders labeled, for example, "horse," "juice," "bread," "home," and "mother." RSCH itself was too busy doing more important things to concern itself with the mundanity of data-sorting.

(And how to discuss RSCH. How not to? Understand that opening my mouth and speaking was speaking RSCH into RSCH, which was speaking myself, which was RSCH—an impossibility, but we were thick with it, and really, in that case, what is there to describe? I'm not one to make sense.)

I say RSCH is a massive skeleton; an array of maze like bones around a hollow space. Imagine each little piece of bone to be one RSCH, and imagine each of these pieces to be reporting to another, who is reporting to another, and on and on and on. They are connected like the sentences of data except I cannot read them. Who is at the top? Is there a top? The only top I know of is Truth, to which they all report and attend; Truth, which they groom Purer than possible. RSCH is Truth, because it is the result of RSCH, which is Truth, and RSCH must be Right and True, because it, in Rightness and Truth, created itself. The truth need not have one voice or even a chorus. It simply is. The data below is no matter, its form meaning little; the objective Real laid roots beneath the insignificant shadows of language.

Better that the truth not be heard at all, only felt. We lived surrounded by it, bordered at our edges by a jagged forest. Before the forest was the Community, beyond it was the wild, and the wild was a dark place that was no-place at all. All of this was RSCH because RSCH centered and surrounded it, RSCH was RSCH everywhere, except the forest ungoverned by RSCH, in which the things RSCH forbade took place according to RSCH mandate.

The RSCH building has a piece of itself everywhere. It is impossibly high and impossibly red and I have heard its basement is long enough to meet the core of the earth like the Truth itself. Citizens see it only in corners. It is the center and the outline of the Community. A piece is in the forest. It is everywhere but we must stay away from it—it can watch but must not be seen in its totality.

The duty of a Citizen to RSCH is first and foremost the duty of memory, that is, to store data for later recall, that is, to use the yet-Impure body as a storage capsule. Our eyes make the data into the plane between the spoke and the world; eye contact is mandatory as it allows us to view another's vitals and social standing. This is why the removal of the contacts is such a grave offense. To remove is to deny service to the RSCH record. We attend school not in order to learn memory but to practice Citizenship, to use our eyes as keys to all knowledge, contacts proving that they fit the lock.

This I write from a distance. My data is gone. I am buried deep into the ground. I don't yet know where. Nowhere.

RSCH issues periodic reports, also contact-accessible. These reports discuss the state of things in the Community. There is the climate-phenomena section, in which the relationship between the woods and our area is assessed

> (although it is all our area, meaning RSCH's area, except that the woods, the wild, is outside RSCH's domain—nothing is outside RSCH's domain, but RSCH does not govern the woods, so   happens there)

And the state of our protective field is discussed. We are updated on potential threats from the wild, new dangers posed by lurking Uncitizens. These threats fall under the climate phenomena section because they are labelled as "pollution."

Lately, the threat of pollution has been especially great. This latest report, according to whomever pirated access to it, has a long list of all the month's Uncitizened, a higher number than the preceding two months combined. The faceless body that relayed this pirate information to me intoned a warning before running off behind the trees. They say the number is rising. *It is reaching epidemic proportions.* **We need all be worried,** RSCH says. **We must remain on our guard: if you see something, say something; report all potential threats to RSCH using the instant-access channel in your AR contacts. Thank you for doing your part.**

The faceless body looked at me solemnly from its smooth, featureless head. I said, "I understand."

I knew such reporting as RSCH described was rare; we deviants did not stray from the wild once defected. No Pure Citizen would have the opportunity to report us. The duty of defilement fell to the sound of the axe. The cracking took up space behind my eyes, a weighty toxin in my skull, a train a train a train a train of thought would not let me go. I lay awaiting Reya's retrieval.

2. Citizenship is zero-sum.

We await the axe.
My least favorite subject.
The one I prevent my mind from thinking. To be a Citizen
is to unmake another, zero-sum. I can only speak of the axe in fragments or.
If pushed,
in a clipped fashion. Like this. Like sentences. Like incomplete.

There can only be so many Citizens before a period is reached.
No one but RSCH knows the number.
It is in the Nature of the Community to remain in balance.
It is in the Nature of RSCH to know the Nature of Nature.
RSCH can end but cannot kill because RSCH is life

From all I had heard, the Recitizenship examination was challenging. It was still more challenging for those whose brains had been washed out, cut up, and hung to dry, as was the case with the patients and eventual axers. Each just-missing swing, a plea to pass. Each failure to cleave some disobedient spine a mark against the deviant subject. And they would be deviant until they found a deviant whose place they could take, whose bleeding body evidenced their compliance.

But even the partial restoration of Citizenship one could not wholly undo a patient's deviant past. Their access to the Network was severely limited. Their stats were exclusively visible to, and closely monitored by, RSCH. Their health margins were tighter. Adults reported daily to be weighed and measured, checked for pulse and blood pressure. Watched as they downed a complete nutritional supplement, blood-tested weekly for nutritional compliance. They were the tangled roots at the core of the poisoned soil which RSCH struggled to fight against.

True Citizens who had never been patients each had holographic cards which read CLASS-I, printed in block letters beside their name and the letter of their chromosomal affiliation, since shortened from a confusing combination of Xes and Ys to the more convenient "F" and "M." CLASS-II Citizens' cards possessed a larger stamp which overlaid their personal details entirely. I do not remember the color of the stamp but only that it was garish, even ugly. Cards were to be carried at all times, especially for CLASS-II Citizens, who risk a prompt stripping of status upon first failure to produce a card when asked. This is not because the absence of a card renders one's details unavailable, but rather because failure to carry a Citizenship card is evidence of Anti-Social Behaviors that render one unsuitable for the Community writ large.

Apart from the cards, CLASS status was always available via AR contacts, except to CLASS-IIs, whose status was visible to CLASS-Is but whose access to others' status was forbidden. A CLASS-I, it is said, must know whether or not they are interacting with a CLASS-II. For a CLASS-II to demand such knowledge was surely a sign of a Ruminatory Personality in need of treatment. Regardless of CLASS, the contacts were mandatory and irremovable. I have had mine out for a significant period of time I remain unable to measure.

There were those who occupied the undifferentiated space between

CLASSes I and II. I was one. It felt as if I were suspended close to the very tops of the wild trees, as the trees themselves caught false-flame.

> RSCH held simulated, controlled burns in order to educate the populace as to the inferiority of pre-Community life. We have similar educative simulations of hunger, thirst, pain, fear, and anger, all also forbidden from Citizen experience.

New axers emerged each day to mark the Bad and make of themselves the Good. Having been educated out of the deviant sensations forbidden to feel, they returned to the mediated world of life.

Every morning I woke and wondered when it would be me. When I would bleed to make life. How many Citizens were stamped and shaped each day. Was there a quota to fill. A limit. I said all of these as if they were facts because there was a RSCH answer somewhere and RSCH was Fact. When I took this line of thought and stretched it by the length of me it was as if an insurmountable wall had fallen and made a new landscape in its rubble. It could fix me to the spot like a stubborn root. **If too many thoughts invade your mind,** occupying its landscape, **you yourself become one of them—infected, a thought to be stopped.**

It was a RSCH teaching, a means of combatting polluted thoughts, invaders of the pristine consciousness of the Citizen. Like the axings, the thought-stoppage is our first line of defense against invaders, the marking of a period against infection. I no longer consciously employ these methods

> they employ me. They are evidence

>> -based. That is to say, they could not be reasonably argued against. That is to say, the arguer would be unreasonable to argue with evidence-based techniques educated into them by RSCH whose evidence is true. To do this would be antisocial, and thus defective.

Thought-stopping worked best when training began young—age three, at the same time as school began. At first, it was a challenge—young children, hardly more than animals, corralled and led toward clarity. It had been this way for several generations before mine, all of whose compliance and agreeableness personality scores rose steadily as intervention age lowered. My mother's intervention age had been five; her mother's, seven. With each two-year downstep, neurotic antagonisms decreased, too, wild social elements contained. The lesson, unambiguous: **thought (is) action, action (does) thought.** To stop thought is to stop collapse.

Thought-stoppage was a simple, low-resource regulatory project, simple to teach but costing a lifetime to master. One was to imagine a sign in hisorher mind and the sign was bright and blinking. The sign was the size of a wall, it could grow and think   and shrink with ease as needed. The sign, the wall, stood between me and the badthought. Every time a badthought attempts to migrate from the great dark beyond, and into the light behind our eyes, we were to construct another sign on top of the already-existing one. Build our defenses.

After enough signs, the wall is solid, heavy, indefatigable. The Community was made of a series of fortified walls that were once and still remain signs. It is simply hard to see from the inside.

In the middle of my education, still before Reya's appearance, a fresh Recitizen was exhibited in our classroom. We had been warned in advance and provided, for the duration of the class, a fortification mod for our AR contacts. Fortify, this was the word   the world   they   made, imbued with strength against enemies in our midst. The fortification update turned Recitizens, CLASS-II Citizens, a fuzzed grey-beige, made them lag in speech and movement. I could watch a body and its lagshadow move in a strange gradient, darkness first concentrated and then fading into air. They would be this way forever, bodies excessive and scrambled. Bodies too body for RSCH, which seek cure   Pure.

Through my childhood contacts, I watched the CLASS-II in our class sway several times before a look of reprimand from our teacher froze him in place.

"Introductions," our teacher had said, and the shadow straightened his shadow body.

"I am called HI-09283, this is my name, as the names of the noncompliant are forsaken." I wanted desperately to know how he looked, even how his true voice sounded, not the one we knew to be scrubbed clean and compliant. He sounded like RSCH. As though RSCH was in his mouth.

"Good morning, HI-09283," we replied in unison, as instructed.

"I am here to talk to you about Citizenship," he said. "As you know, the Citizen carries a body. These bodies we must shoulder, maintain. We maintain the body through practices of restraint and compliance.

"I am the result of failed compliance. My repeated, untreated failures to thoughtstop leaked from the heights of my mind to the low depths of my body. In the depths, my body became unmanageable. I have behaved animally, though, thanks to my Recitizenship training, I have been spared the details of my animality so as to avoid reinfection."

It was at this point that I began to shiver. I am shivering. I looked up at our teacher, expecting a glare or perhaps a verbal reprimand for impermissible movement. I noticed, then, that my classmates were shivering, too: each of us vibrated at the intensity of HI's story, this proximity to deviance, this violent wrongbodied encounter.

"This is a test," I overheard our teacher say. Heard, over the vibrations which had now become a buzz. "These details of deviance tempt you. You may want to attempt access to the Imagination. What have we learned to do when the desire arises—"

STOP   A sudden darkness. I am at the dinner table.

Thought-stopping was one of the most difficult roadblocks for defectives to bypass on the path to Recitizenship. Why. Why? The axe was simply not enough **to return them to us**, although I am not us, but them, but I speak as us and I use that voice I don't—**STOP**   See. I try to keep up with my doing this so that in the case that I am next I might stand a chance and like HI, return to Us.

Have you ever felt yourself becoming a *them* but even as the distance grows between you and *us*—the Citizens—you find great pleasure, great comfort in pretending for a moment that you are still of *us*? That you are still safe; that there are still others below you on whose hisorher faces you step on on your walks around town? Is this what *us* is, this refusal, this stepping? The small mercy that there are still things in the shadows that are hated more than you?

i'm the future im
possibility learning not to fear
itself, the future
of the body of the
im little
lost fingers, lazed
tumorous a cross
between
a cyborg since the words
made me and a

i submit in the face of the scalpel
in the face of the truth of the law of
of the bed of the sight of i grind
against.

I could tell a CLASS-II Citizen from a CLASS-I, even unfortified, but not with my mother's accuracy.

I couldn't tell it about Reya, but then, Reya was never a CLASS-II. They were no one at all.

My mother always claimed she could smell the CLASSes, said so whenever we saw a bunch of strangers in the supermarket. This is false because RSCH tells us Citizens have no smell and to perceive a smell where there is not a smell is delusion. Citizens, in truth, have almost no sense of smell, nor any reason to have one. Our senses of smell and taste have been dulled in favor of the superior senses, sight and sound, and because we need fear no food nor predator. **We need not have the non-senses of animals, those long-gone pests whose behaviors deviants mimic in their-**our **forest hideaways**. What my mother detected was a difference in movement. An extra over-shoulder glance, a stumble. Whenever this would happen she would send a message through the contacts, jostling my brain so I could not look away. We would pick up our nutritional shakes, appearing silent but in fact deep in conversation. Another message: *avoid*. Avoid becoming, avoid associating. I'd nod almost-imperceptibly. If she didn't catch it she'd send another message with the Loud affect so that I'd know she was serious, and we'd exit the supermarket together with our cart of shake boxes. I'd take special care to walk like a natural Citizen walked, though I was one already.

All the while I'd remember them. Pasty regardless of complexion, all the light stripped from their faces and then seemingly-reapplied haphazard and fluorescent. As if they could not walk and then regained the ability and now stumbled like children. Their heads would tilt to this side and that, as if listening for instructions. Maybe they were. All I knew for sure is that my mother's eyes were perpetually-open to the nearest CLASS-II, mouth ready to whisper "another," and pupils poised to type a similar message. Then, she'd turn to them surreptitiously, blink, and record an image to inspect more closely later.

My own method for determining CLASS was different. I could not see CLASS in their gait, but in their ghost. It was an indescribable thing, and thus, a dangerous one, one for which there was no RSCH language and thus one which did not, on a practical level, exist. Yet I saw it when they flashed stamped-over identification at the register. I saw it on their starch-white clothing and in the way they give CLASS-I Citizens the bulk of the aisle space, moving themselves and their carriage around us in wide skittish arcs, as if their trundling, fortified shadow remained. I felt them watching us when they believed we weren't looking back. We all played along and did not look back until their own backs were turned, lest we see something in them and become   They, on the rare occasions our eyes met, turned ghostly at the sight of our contacts. Slowly we would both turn away and, retrieving the supplement from one of many identical shelves, making our way to the register with crates of sustenance.

> Supplements supplemented a well-existence ensured already by biopsychosocial hygiene by providing the nutrients required to sustain and reproduce a balanced lifestyle.

While technically unnecessary, trips to the supermarket encouraged prosocial activity. The shared experience of picking up supplements contributed to harmony within the Community via shared engagement in approved activity. Missing a week's pickup was not automatic grounds for assessment, but a pattern of antisocial behavior—in this case, exclusive trips to work or school without appropriate unstructured socialization—put individuals in the category of High Risk. Their AR files, including their SmartFile™ memories, would be bumped to the head of RSCH's data-assessment queue. Their vital stats were reviewed with increasing regularity, their ability to engage in appropriate self-conduction in public space under increased scrutiny.

CLASS-II Citizens were particularly keen to use the supermarket as a demonstration of pro-social abilities. They flocked to public areas, eager in their attempts to network with CLASS-Is, compensating for their limited AR contacts. If at some point a CLASS-II attempted to innate conversation, few CLASS-Is, particularly children, might stop for a moment and listen. CLASS-Is were advised to keep at least the length of one adult's arm between themselves and CLASS-IIs.

My mother never let us stop, but once recorded me for public reprimand when I moved to close to a CLASS-II. She had been speaking so earnestly, seeking only recognition. "Do you see me," she had asked. "I just want to know you can see me." I had walked up close, hardly a hand away. Her eyes, bare in the absence of comprehensive contacts, scoured me for data, as if we are Networked together once more, as if we make a litany of stacked memories all made of our respective pairs of eyes.

"It is our duty—our responsibility—to keep them at arm's length," said my mother. "We must look, not indulge a need to be seen." She could smell even then my own deviant eyes. My inability to look without sight.

To give the sense of place. To give the sense of being-in. To give tense, to give tension.

At the limit of woods words and grammar the trees' grammar made possible.

We made third options to manage what was left
of our bodies, mostly with the help of the Operator.

The Operator, like the woods, was outside words.

It was not from RSCH, nor was it a Citizen, nor was it specifically a deviant,
although it made us possible with its lone and indiscernible body and unspeakable parts.

To our knowledge, the Operator had never been a Citizen, deviant, RSCH, or any other conceivable sort of consciousness, so it went by *it*, as an event or phenomenon might. It used thin, unbreakable fibers to knot our open wounds into submission. These fibers held my stomach and third arm in place. They held Reya's crutches to their forearms tightly but allowed them to be released easily and at will.

Reya usually slept without their crutches. At the lately then, they remained attached. That is, prepared to run. This did not stop us from any of our nightly activities.

At this moment I am in a tree, attempting to recount all of this to the best of my ability before I fall asleep. I am not in a tree but make myself into the memory of a tree. This is all not ready to understand yet.

●

At the time of this tree we'd just gotten our newest crate of hormone supplements, secreted, somehow, from RSCH stores

Citizens who were irregularly male-or-female, deficient in some mild, treatable sense, took them at RSCH's prescription, and were marked, alongside all manner of deviants, as "CLASS-II": Citizens, but only just. Citizens, contingent upon the clinic.

Injection of a Citizen with a foreign chemical is under all circumstances forbidden, **criminal contamination**. When RSCH injected hormones they were not foreign chemicals but supplements to the body that should have been, and thus they were permitted. For the rest of us, self-given and unmonitored injections constituted self-hacking, in the form of self-mutilatory behaviors, which counted among the most dangerous of the deviancies.

RSCH could not hack, because hacking was crime and RSCH was law. RSCH could not mutilate because RSCH did no harm.

I was never hormone-deficient, yet I took the hormones because I needed them, covering myself   in needlesized holes. The woods was where I learned it all, how to desecrate the RSCH property which was myself. It was where I first learned how to shrug off my parole.

(p)erforming of (a) (role), our role, in the Community; to act in a way which adhered to RSCH outcomes. Doing a body appropriately, that is, transcending it. With the dr, parole. School, work: parole. Walking or sitting in the street were both parole. With the contacts, parole continued when we were all alone, which we were not.

I was never hormonally deficient, but I took the supplements because I needed them. That is, I was not a patient of the hormones but took them monthly after our walk to the base of the distributive area. This was always a frightening process. We relied on the unspeakable and unnamable and unmappable on which we tread, or did not tread, because we were no-place, and as no-place, no-time: I knew, thanks to Reya, that the supplements could be keepers—of time, of gates, of bodies   of law. Yet on arrival, they are stripped, as are we: hardly clothed in the glamour of Truth, out of time.

Why did I do it. I did it in part because I could. I did it in part because they, the hormones, made me feel something. I couldn't say if it was the pinprick, the sensation of thick, clear fluid entering my thigh, the spots of blood that lingered and drooled and dried in the breeze. I didn't know if it was the pleasurable taste of blood I snuck with every poke. I did it for other reasons, too, those I didn't know how to name. I did it because I liked the sharpness of my chin, the hair dusting my jaw, and even the plump red beads that grew and later burst across my face. I liked that when I murmured, I murmured differently, a difference I could feel in my ribs. I liked it when I knew I was doing them angrily, as if each pump was a scream in the language of disobedience. Forbidden feelings for forbidden chemicals. Sometimes it felt like all the anger I had ever felt had been locked inside the shots the distributor gave us, just waiting there for me, as if I defected by design.

For fifteen RSCH years or so, right into the center of my adolescence, RSCH had my body as RSCH wanted it. At midnight of the new year, upon which all Community members aged, all turning-twelve girls would begin attending periodic egg-extractions. Likewise with the boys and their sperm. All of us, boys and girls, would grow in all the unspeakable requisite ways the body must grow in order to achieve adulthood. While monitored remotely via the contacts, our data was regularly reviewed during in-person appointments at the RSCH clinics, whose individual outposts were located with predictable frequency around the Community. Each clinic looked like a large beige box, entirely windowless. The smooth surface allowed for much AR engagement for patients waiting to be seen. (When unsighted by the dr, the patient did not exist).

RSCH measures health holistically. Only the body whose physiological, productive, and psychosocial data and metadata

> (the data accumulated on us as we worked with RSCH data, which, we acknowledged, could be the very same data that was being accrued for our file for review, but because all was in code, no one knew if that they worked with was being invented in real time, and their acknowledgement of its invention was the thing that made it,

> But RSCH is all

> that can declare the data real, and that is why it's encoded, because we cannot be trusted with the stuff, and so instead we live a life of **uncertainty-tolerance**, which is the disciplinary mechanism we learn in order to better submit to RSCH while maintaining a **stable civic attitude**).

was ascertained to be normal were cleared as healthy Citizens. The absence of one health marker, just one, indicated holistic contamination, much like one deviant within a Community could slowly, surely infect the mass.

Besides houses, then, clinics were the most common structures within the communities. There was one clinic for every five-hundred Citizens, and within each clinic were twenty-five offices. Citizens were scheduled for routine check-ups once per month.

There were also the non-routine appointments, which used the back-door of the windowless offices, one the normal patient need never see. I witnessed one when I was twelve, getting my measurements taken at a monthly visit in order to ensure my achievement of adolescent womanhood. I was stiff and cold in my white undergarments. Between bust and waist measurements I heard a strange noise on the other side of the office's wall-to-wall mirror, to which I stood parallel. My mother and examiner were there, too; my mother sat opposite the mirror taking notes on the dr's observations, and the dr herself thought aloud in snipped little Truths as she attended to my body—here is your pointed knee, too pointed, I can feel the bone; here is your hip, which has failed to widen. Both acted as if they could hear nothing, despite the increasing volume of the sounds.

This was my cue to behave as they did. Just as I at the time attempted to obey the demand not to look in the wall-to-wall mirror, for fear of engaging in **ruminative self-image-seeking behavior**, I also attempted not to react to the sound. I attempted to unsound the sound, to remind my mind that I could not be trusted. As my examiner directed me to remove my underwear in order to complete the examination, the sound grew even louder than before. My mother turned away from me, not in response to the sound, which was not a sound, but because no Citizen but an office dr was permitted to see another Citizen over the age of six fully nude.

I took the time away from my mother's eyes to look, briefly, in the mirror. The mirror became a window. I saw the sound.

I saw a large, smooth, wholly indescribable piece of equipment with an open back, as if ready to be filled. I tuned my ears to the sudden sound of human voices, a sound whose source I didn't know. One voice was of an adolescent my age, a girl, and the other must have been the dr. You could tell a RSCH voice the way **it stuck in your head like a weight** and so I felt it instantly inside, a face bold and expanding until it was too big to contain and I believed my stomach, my chest, my face about to explode.

The girl was screaming. "What did you do with them? Where did they go? How much did you take?" I had never heard a scream before. It was a negative behavior. This one hurt my ears and head.

I stared into the mirror and listened to the silence of the RSCH dr. I didn't know where I was anymore, but I was not in the office in which I was being examined. I was floating, untethered and vague, just outside the scene.

The unsound sound of the scream continued. It waxed and waned as the girl's head swung this way and that. After a period, several other drs entered the space and, in gloved hands, lifted not only her body but the entire apparatus. Her body was remarkably, dangerously, hatefully small, as if her scream were all concentrated directly at her center.

The girl was shouting for her mother. The mother stood still by her side, placid as her daughter was dragged away. She commented at her daughter's fading body: "It is not responsible to harbor this kind of activity in my home. Do you want me to be punished for *your* deviance?"

"THIS WAS FAKE. THIS WAS A TRAP. I KNEW THIS WAS THE WRONG DAY AND YOU TRAPPED ME." I noticed that the girl's hair was deep red, a rare color given her golden-brown complexion. Her bones poked at wild angles through her paper-skin and outlines of veins rose from her wrists. She had no breasts, it seemed, although surely they lurked somewhere beneath her jutting ribs.

This was the first problem. The breasts should have bulged by now but the bones did instead. I watched as she was dragged out the back door to be loaded—off to where? Defectives whose blighted bodies failed to change appropriately were treated accordingly in RSCH headquarters, I knew this. Most often, their apparent inability to develop appropriately was related to recent gender disobedience, sometimes to miscellaneous physiological non-compliances. I did not know the precise treatment. I simply knew it happened elsewhere.

"**IF YOU DO NOT COMPLY YOU WILL NOT BECOME A WOMAN, YOU WILL BECOME NOTHING.**" The RSCH boomed. It stuck. The emboldened words stuck to her body and bled through her skin. The patient continued her twisting, although it was less violent now, text-sub-dued. More text, more bleeding, and I reminded myself mid-observance that I was still looking into a mirror, still seeing something that could as easily be an imagining by my own head. (My head did things to the truth of my body like this. Unspeakable and deviant things.)

"I don't want to," moaned the patient. Her eyes were rimmed with red and leaked violent tears. "Please, I'll be quiet—I don't need anything—just let me go."

"**AND STEAL WHAT COULD BE A HEALTHY BODY FROM THE COMMUNITY?**"

Her pores opened, sucked the words in, bulging where they melted. Breasts came out of her arms, her sternum, gurgling with the sick of the ink. The drs moved their hands steadily downwards, until her hands flew to theirs, ripping them from her flesh. She had stricken them. She had touched a dr, though drs could not be touched.

"MISPLACED-AGGRESSION. SELF-DENIAL. SELF-HACK-ING (BIO-TYPE)."

I saw her in the mirror. Then, above her, saw myself. Saw her again and she was back in the drs hands, being whisked away. She faded into nothingness and her mother watched her go, her tiny body, enribbed, shrinking to a grey-white point. The drs who had loaded and disappeared her returned to the inside of the clinic as if nothing was the matter. And so it was: she was the matter and she was nothing.

Her drs disappeared from my view after that, no doubt entering some RSCH-only space still inaccessible to me. The mother had evaporated as soon as the scene was through. All at once I was back in the examination room, called by the sound of snapping fingers.

What's the matter with you? Attention. Attention. Where did your eyes go.

My eyes had gone to Where, it seemed, an impermissible place. My pupils touched hers and she read me.

Satisfied, she said, **You were looking in the mirror**. I had been, but her say-so made it True. She jabbed a gloved hand toward the offending object, myself, before moving to point to the glass. We had the misfortune to live, still, in the body, which was to be honed as we prepared for transcendence. We were to *fix* but not fixate upon the body, perfect it without perfectionism, mirror the selves we would be without the body with the very bodies we were shedding. This is why we needed RSCH help, such a task could not be accomplished by mere Citizens. The bodies failing this were a blight. A festering wound. This carted-off girl no doubt full of holes.

Healing, it seemed, was a trap difficult to escape, even harder to surreptitiously resist. But the wounded hole could be a truth through which the other leaked. My making, I thought toward the mirror, was to fester it.

●

Hormones, like other illicit materials, always arrived in feasts and famines,

> a mythic term connoting the dangerous imbalance of pre-RSCH societies, when feelings and supplies and even tempera-tures were unpredictable.

though I could not remember a famine quite so bad as this one. The Distributor had not come for a very long time; the Operator's stash of spare parts was running low. Word had been circu-lating of a RSCH crackdown on hormone theft, a crackdown which was not actually happening, because RSCH eliminated self-hacking generations ago. Still, we self-hackers, once able to traipse through darkness to find chemical crates on the other side of it, now found few tools for evasion.

Rumor was that ink, the most important of the illicit materials, would be next to go. Once used alongside wood byproducts as an archiving tool, ink defuncted the contacts, defected us, cut us off so that when we went to the woods our precise location could not be traced. From Reya, I had learned that RSCH, before becoming RSCH, had once used ink to convert the last of the anti-contact holdouts in the final moments before the new tech became mandatory. Those who refused the contacts were blinded, slated for elimination. Their communities were mapped, that is, enclosed without pos-sible escape. (Those who defected made up the first of the forest.)

Even now, there was was a chance of being blinded by the inking. The blinded ones I'd met in passing seemed unbothered, though, describing newfound visions of pattern, color, and light, of splattered ink suspended in space. It was a stunning dance of shapes in ten thousand formations that was said to dot the corners of their view, turning their sight from a predict-able landscape to a maze of wonder and contradiction. They claimed to see things RSCH could not see, and that this was the point. I believed them. But I remembered, too, the old RSCH ad we studied in school, a reminder of a disenlightened past. To my frustration, every time I saw someone who saw differently, I saw that old RSCH ad in which anti-contact communities persevered:

> There was the teenage boy, crying out of blackened, mutilated eyes, the girl being restrained so gently by two RSCH hands while she

attempts to scratch out her blackened eyes. The tagline was always **Let yourself make contact.**

The ad stuck with me. I was afraid when I was first inked. I feared the possibility of darkness that seemed to pour from the tiny black vial in front of me. No, I feared the loss of the light whose RSCH-promise I still hung to, afraid of all the places light could not reach. I was afraid of becoming one of those places. When I yessed the ink, for a moment, I was one. My vision clouded briefly, then cleared. All had a violet hue. I clenched my teeth and wondered whether I would see in violets forever, if all the wild deviants really saw in violets and hadn't thought to tell me. I never asked. Perhaps I see in violence.

But soon my eyes the violence cleared and I saw in every color. I saw no AR indicators, no black reminders of my body. I began to cry from my new eyes and I drank the tears that fell into my mouth. Citizens were forbidden from crying, so I cried harder, half-believing the ink had carried some **Irrational Emotive Tendencies** from my eyes to brain and now, now, here I was, a deviant, without hope—

> Of course, I **was a deviant without hope**. I was sitting in the dirt with no clothes on. I was grateful the Operator's face did not have eyes so I would not have to watch it looking at me. I was not, however, immune from Reya's withering gaze.

"Why so scared of losing your eyes, when we already know we're past-people anyway. Would you be afraid of losing your *legs*, too?" Reya had demanded just before my inking. They shifted their weight for emphasis, slightly adjusting their crutches.

"I know," I said. Back then I was still a little bit afraid to look directly at their stumps. I was afraid to see what they meant. I couldn't tell, either, what they meant by *past-people*: whether they referred to us as similar to people from the past (who I had always learned of in caricature) or instead that we had passed personhood somewhere, and the lives we lived now were lived in the wake of who we were. I supposed I was used to my name and any other, even a positive one, was a great upset. Past-person. Passed-person. Whatever I was, I certainly didn't pass. Was I living in the past? Could I be turned around to? I continued continued until I **STOPPED** the thought.

I was a defective, a deviant, an Uncitizen. It was most useful to use the terms I had learned for myself, even before I became myself. It was useful to use them without fuss or ceremony. It was frightening to hear myself an unfamiliar name, but it also made me wonder just what RSCH did when it did our **RSCH VOICES** to us. Whose filter to speak a self through, whose filter refuses violet. Ink fresh, thoughts swarmed me. Stop. Swarm. I ignored myself until I succeeded. When I had healed enough, Reya and I ventured away from the Operator and spoke of practical matters, as if outside time there was a beginning.

Reya had stumps which rounded off into soft, curved caps at the mid-thigh. The stumps had been carefully concealed while we were in the Community, attending school, and if they hadn't shown me someday someplace outside spacetime I would never have noticed the prostheses that stood in for their legs, so convincing, the warm brown of their flesh so well-matched, and the shape of muscle articulated so precisely, that they may as well have been real, that is, the result of RSCH.

The shock of the legs, or lack of them, had at first profoundly disturbed me. RSCH produced only real subjects, whose data was whole and complete. We were directed to tolerate the unknown with the knowledge that it was Known to RSCH, arbiters of Truth, and that assurance that this Truth was known and true sufficed in place of knowledge. Indeed, the knowledge that Truth was Knowledge itself was knowledge enough for the Citizen, for whom any attempt to grasp at the knowing itself suggested a pathological need for control.

> RSCH use of the contacts to reckon a Citizen's heart-rate, blood pressure, weight, height, body temperature, step count, movement pace, blood sugar, testosterone, estrogen, progesterone, serotonin, and cortisol was not indicative of pathology because RSCH makes ideal health.

In these projects, full Citizen compliance is necessary to ensure Community wholeness. Doubtless, the most vital data sits within those who seek to withhold it. This seemed to be the case with bodies. It was the case with Reya's. They blended as a Citizen in impossible ways. They couldn't have passed a home EyeScan bank (wherein retinal imaging functioned as what was once called a "key"[2] and which ensured all who ink are not permitted covert return) nor would they have made it through the clinic. But they came to school and passed the days as if they were a house among the houses that were students there, each architecturally consistent, identically-painted, predictable so as to yield positive mental health outcomes.

Still Reya was wild at the root. Born deviant, they had no option.

---

2 Contemporary, correct usage of the word "key" refers to any social interconnection facilitated by the contacts. To send or receive a Network notification is to key or have been keyed. RSCH keys into our vital statistics through the interpretation of data.

Their acts of camouflage (the term used to describe the crime of Truth-obfuscation), in fact, reinforced the power of their deviation, and their being found out for what they were was a matter of time as long as they remained in the Community. When they went to return I came by their side. I went by their side. I am confused as to coming and wenting and where am I here.

It was not so difficult to stay in the wild, so long as one could run or crutch or somehow move quickly. It was, however, difficult to *went*, to defect under the translucent cover of a night whose darkness was by law never complete, nor even overwhelming. Streetlights at all hours, powered by the sun in whose gaze our ancestors once cowered. Now, the sun obeyed RSCH alone; soon, they would conquer not the sun but the body and the certain itself. Until such an escape was possible, the lights would keep is Known, that is, encased   in   cased. The Curfew, the nightly pill, kept us asleep. The contacts' maps revealed no anti-RSCH path; such spaces were unreal.

> We unfound them ourselves.
> Exited the boundary unfindable.
> Located unplace no map. I
> don't know how and won't tell.
> On nightfall, walking, running,
> darking, between the lights and
> outward not here. No words
> RSCH this.

How would we escape curfew? Stay away awake between streetlights, escape the map by the method of not knowing how. I don't know how I did it, even now. Only RSCH mapmakes. Everywhere and nowhere; in the air and the soil. RSCH uncontaminated but in possession of the wilds yet marking the wilds out of reach. How to get away. We must walk behind it.

Once in the wilds, uncontacted, I learned to move again. There was no criminality checker installed in my eyes, and knowing my eyes were inked I no longer looked at myself quite so closely. I could not go home. Home was no longer a place that applied to me. Yet without a home, without a law to call my own, I felt I had stepped into someplace new. I could be a non-someone, perhaps the only way to leave what it means to be known.

The wilds are vast but finite. There were many spaces I never got to see. On our normal route, Reya and I would pass the edge of the hormone path, which we walked with the Operator and others periodically to the distribution zone. We would enter the thick of the rejected area, whose ground is thick with limbs and hearts and fungi. There were weeds as tall as I was. There was rancid ancient tech whose uses I could only guess, tech that had once been attached to the people who had once unexisted and now remained here. And there were the bodies. In their pieces.

They are what haunted everything, shadows in the distance like flags to mark the boundary between Community and elsewhere. They I am among, or was. You can't expect my grammar when the bodies are strewn, an arm and a leg and one of that arm's hand's fingers all out of place. The grammar to tell that in the shadow of the real of the highlit truth. I would wander through the bodies and sometimes sit among them, making my own body like a corpse and imagining in pieces.

Beside me, an arm made of wood, carved, I could tell, with delicacy. On the other side, an organ long sapped of its juices, a husk of its former self, surrounded by a small ring of mushrooms. It was difficult to tell which ones you should eat and which make you sick, but then, in the wilds I am always sick.

to steal
the weapon. body
to steal away to hid
ing, to steal at last
the last red dregs
a pool of blue.

notathing but dark its absence
a trail so black it's anti-path

3. CRIMINAL BODILY ACTIVITY.

It goes like this. We make it, with the help of the Operator, to the door. The dispenser opens the door, has with it a pallet of bottles. The bottles are each labelled with one or more of several symbols whose significance and meaning are unknown. We each take a pallet or more, unless we can't, in which case we move to some place in the line of deviants as a lookout. People have been axed out here. We are so especially close to RSCH. I swear I can hear the heartbeat of the thing, an organism itself even as it transcends the body. I know they can hear my own.

Just before it all happened—just after this present I am telling you about, this tense tense I write feel—a report came out of RSCH. I saw it projected on the sky, just like the rest. This one read:

RESURGENCE OF ANTITRUTH ACTIVITY THREATENS THE SAFE SANE SANCTITY OF OUR COMMUNITY

AFTER A DANGEROUS RESURGENCE OF CRIMINAL BODILY ACTIVITY WE KINDLY DEMAND ALL THOSE ON SECTION A-F HOR-MONE REGULATION REGIMENS TO REPORT TO THEIR BODILY HYGIENE DEPARTMENT FOR IMMEDIATE EVALUATION

When the message came out, we all sensed something different, something more serious than the periodic threats to the supply we'd felt before. We could tell this time was different because they publicly acknowledged the specific letter-labelled regimens we stole. They had avoided doing so before, preferring to clip silently the wounds from the collective's body, which would remain pristine only with this constant, conscious pruning. Even Reya was surprised at that new report—this admission to what was known and not-known, believed yet not True, true yet unspeakable. The admission that the wounds had left a mark, that Purity, in having been violated, was under threat of violation.

When the body is a sacred site, it is as powerful as it is vulnerable. Invincible yet threatened. The corrupted body did not exist for precisely the same reasons it—we—made it to the woods. Ink the eyes, eliminate the contacts. Use the hormones recklessly, grow on

themselves fuzz or flesh prohibited,

become bodies

unrecognizable as Citizen.

Then suddenly you were a threat that never was, lurking in the shadow of the Real, the Truth of which you may well have still believed.

The greatest difficulties, the greatest obstacles to overcome, are the ideas the Commission —RSCH—puts into your head. The idea that Pure bodies could do things that corrupted bodies could not; that contamination destroys and does not create anew in its place. That there is nothing beyond the Imagination.

On the march to the Distributor we made ourselves the shadows. Scouts watched for errant axers, sometimes for extended periods: deviants, many of us new defectors, were unused to strenuous exercise, perspiration, and even pain. All were part of the walk. I reveled in it, my back bowed to the bottles of sensation to which I ow(n)ed myself. I walked until my body, hot and cold and damp, gave way to the black spots at the edges of my vision, an ink unto itself, and Reya would say "we're done walking for the night," but I would continue into it until the night itself forced me into the earth.

●

Reya is gathering fruit, lurching through high, uncut weeds that look like ugly NewGrass replicas. I squint until I notice a fading trail of Reyas behind my own, their copyselves are catching on the weeds and hanging there, awaiting collection. I see their nose in profile, a brutal, pointed beak. Their hand flies suddenly to the back of their neck. They bow and I can nearly feel the ache of their chip. Then, a sound removes them from their pain and me from my observation.

The event occurs as it always does. Reya acts first. They dig each arm forward, turn by turn, abandoning their fruits and roots among the grasses. Soon they are out of sight.

I know to run. The safest is in the trees themselves; below the ground will also do; in the water is, perhaps, the wisest. I see Reya for a moment, ripping off their garment and plunging into the water, thick and still and murk-laden, but unmatched in its ability to conceal a body, its crutches, and any movement from either despite a relatively shallow depth.

Whoever's running with the axe is closer now. Closer to me. I'm climbing. It's impossible to climb so high while wielding such an unwieldy weapon. This hopes me safe. Axes are absurd; primitive; doers of a violence long-dead. I climb higher. Reya does not so much as bubble in the water when I look back for them. Again I'm looking back. My mistake. I saw the axe-wielder. The axe swashes back and forth and I am stuck   to   it. The sound. The racing image. Thoughts tumble in, dooming, domeing, a hill to pull me to its center, a rush of wind and water faster and faster, dragging me inside,   swing

swing. I imagine Reya screaming. I imagine it so well they started screaming in my ear, but it was not them. I imagine it so well their mouth a   my mouth and pouring blood

●

Death became real in the wild. In the Community, it was just **go-ing-away**. We learned about it in school: before RSCH made health objective and objective health we would die of all manner of deviancy. Disease. Injury. Violence. War.

> This was what fueled the continuous threat of contamination: the invasion of the outside, the dead world, the world that had degenerated into nothing, entering the Community and destroying us from inside.

All four, identical. All four now gone-away with the rest of the gone-away. It seemed living close to death was something our Community just did not do—we were health, we were vibrancy, we were fullness, never hunger; lightness, never dark. Use of the word "death" on the Network was not illegal, but would flag the users interacting with the word as potential actants of inappropriate behaviors requiring immediate medical attention. When a going-away occurred it only occurred if authorized, and the routine for the rest was recovery. Moving on. Re-cover the bodies as if we sat among the barbaric passed past   and used tools to dig the dirt and put ourselves inside it like soiled animals.

We began learning about recovery before understanding what was to be recovered from. Grief had, before RSCH, reached epidemic proportions, in sighting deviancies everywhere. I hear they grieved many Citizens and even *things*. Progress stalled as everyone wept up in it. RSCH took charge in the time of devastation and set us forward. Still some remained**If you witness someone who may be overcome by grief-induced behaviors, please take a HoloScan of at least 33% of hisorher face and submit it to the appropriate authorities. Use the HoloCamera**

> hollow camera red
>
> read   eyes

> **located in your AR contacts for maximum efficiency.**
>
> **Simply call to mind the need embedded in each of us to root out others in our midst.**
>
> **Every Citizen's actions make RSCH**

The radical mourners were the disruptive deviants from way back in the early days. Learning about them made us suspicious of each other. Me, too. Grief seemed outside quantity, uncountable and therefore wild. That meant we could all be harboring it without knowing precisely what or how to measure. We were eight years old. Still always already looking for things amiss. I made mental note of classmates' deviant behavior before I knew what I was doing.

Better.

We are each responsible for preventing cultural-behavioral contagions. Citizen watchfulness is our first line of defense against vectors.

As we see through our study of the psychologically-unhinged "radical mourners' group," overwhelm-by-grief has serious and lasting impacts on one's psyche that have proven treatment-resistant. These include, most importantly, heightened paranoia and a misunderstanding of the linear nature of time. Attempts at recovery appear salubrious when applied to those suffering from emotionally damaged perspectives, and may help to re-integrate the disturbed into civil life.

Within a day of reading one of those grief warnings, someone would, inevitably, not show up at school. Heorshe would undergo testing because someone saw their misbehavior and reported them to the authorities. Sometimes it was a false alarm. Other times, the reported-on student would come up positive for another form of pathology, often one which presented similarly to grief, but distinct enough to warrant a separate diagnosis. It would be said that the report was a happy accident. We all behaved best in the immediate aftermath of one of our number leaving. Of course we did not grieve them. No grief with the situation, no anger, only peace; no incivility, just gratitude. Grief and rage were the bodies expelled from home. The classmates now no more.

If we grieve things that are dead, and we call things dead when they are taken away from us, then I am dead to myself and perhaps to anyone reading this, too. And I am writing this for the public record.

There is no need for grief. There is no

There is memory. There is my memorying down the document and there is making later for it.

4. A long white space.

Think about the present, if it's there.
All different right now. More on the background soon, I believe,
from the space I sit
behind time
's eyelid.

A long white space takes up my entire field of vision. My eyes in a
permanent state of semi-openness. I can feel them drooling. I am neither
sleeping nor waking and deeply uncomfortable to be in the middle   of it. I
am searching for the energy to think about Reya, about the before, although
with every passing moment the act of remembering turned to losing. I imagined the pain was written on my face. Every time a dr entered the room
heorshe would open hisorher mouth in mock-surprise, take a note, disappear.

Periodically one would sit down on a stool beside my bed, typing
on a holographic keyboard, suspended silver and shining in the air. The dr
would stared up at it, at what to himorher, undoubtedly, was a set of charts,
but to me was a vague silvery twinkle of that of mine which was drs' which
was not mine   to know.

"I am getting more tired every day," I said to the dr. This time I
could speak. I felt sore, though I had no recollection of having left the bed
since   I arrived.

"I think things are atrophying," I continued, and then instantly re-
gretted it. My voice squeaked unpleasantly, a pair of discordant tones ground
against each other.

He (I identified this in his rough, low voice before I could think it)
laughed. His face remained blurry. His fuzzy edges shook as he emitted the
sound. My own voice rung back in my head, a fractured accusation.

"Who taught you that word?"

An image of the Operator rushed my head. It used a lot of words like that, ones pirated from drs, ones it had to teach the rest of us. I attempted to **STOP** the image, but before I could hold the memory back, something slipped. I emitted it. What I had been thinking was now gone and the more I dug to grasp it, the further it went.

The laugh. The voice. The question. It was all another trap, an admission   of guilt. Why would he have spoken to me if not to extract something? We were not normally addressed at all, to do so would be to confer a credibility no non-RSCH could attain. I should have said weakening; something unRSCH, something plain.

"I'm just really tired," I said.

"That's because you've gone so long without a shake," he said calmly, still typing. "Are you aware that we require the supplement thrice daily for the sake of our collective health, and that for every Citizen who disobeys, we, collectively, become weaker?"

He produced a bottle from behind his stool. I was not a Citizen, but was in this case. I didn't know that the absence of the supplement could cause this ache in my legs, this tiny, tearing, taring soreness in my ankles. But from his mouth, it was Truth, and I said nothing in response.

Still I squirmed from the bottle. At home the shake would be taken from a tall glass created precisely for that purpose. Here, the thick brown substance was not first poured into a glass but taken directly from the bottle.

dr leaned over me, becoming a shadow on my face. He tipped the thing. The shake was drunk. I felt it sloshing in my first stomach, waiting to be absorbed. My second stomach might as well have disappeared, though I still had the vague sensation of its brushing against the rest of me. The shake grew hands that dug deep into my gut, pushing my spine backward and through my skin, into the bed, and I could not move. No, not the shake. Something else entirely.

All around me glowed a faint blue. Then the light began to dim.

I tried to remember how it felt to run, simulating what lightness I could, but I lost each scene I imagined nearly as soon as it came
The more I do to remember, the more I sense myself being forgotten, turned to something stripped and empty. I saw the edge of the third dimension from my two-dimensional space, flattened against the mattress.

●

Citizens learn early that **the mirror lies**.

It lies because it lets us believe we see ourselves when we cannot. It lies because it tells us each the story we want to hear, when the Truth of our bodies is contained solely in RSCH documents, quantified by stats accessible by the contacts. To look at the body through such an unreliable glass became so taboo it was nearly (though not yet) outright illegal.

To seek one's truth was disobedient to Truth.

We could anticipate it to be so in the future, definitionally superior to the past, which time—in its linear fashion—ran away from,

And as time ran, things became more illegal, because things became more perfect. Time was a process of flight

from imperfection

and one day, the lies

the   mirror tells—lies

imbibed   like toxins

will be no longer –

Until the time that it would become entirely illegal, Citizens had mirror covers for their homes. They could be customized but never uninstalled. The reflective surface reflected a presumption of our authority to reflect on ourselves and the cover was a sign both of self-restraint and of trust in RSCH.

Which was RSCH because we could not access it, because RSCH was secret, because we were not authorized to know it.

RSCH had our patent. They made us   property. They had the exclusive ability to invent—interpret—the Citizen body; we couldn't do so without permission. Mirror-covers were moral imperatives, respecting them a sign of grace. My mother installed an EyeScanner somewhere behind the mirror in our home, which had been covered already by some old white sheets. Now that EyeScanners were becoming cheaper and cheaper, we all started buying them in earnest and using them to accessorize our houses. The scanner would detect the naked eyes of anyone who dared remove the ersatz curtain to get a look in that mirror. The poor soul who decided to sneak a peak would be met with an explosion of sound and color. The AR embedded into the mirror would show a grotesque cartoon creature in lieu of your true reflection. Floating above it would read either:

DO YOU HAVE SOMETHING TO HIDE?

or

WHY ARE YOU RUNNING FROM THE TRUTH?

Public shaming was a highly effective deterrent for Citizens. Though it did not work for me.

I have a troubled relationship with mirrors. It started before the appointment where I stared through at the girl, the dragging. It's a matter of control, of the feeling, continuously, of being held by an invisible fist (albeit a fist that could enter into view at any moment). I cannot accept that I am a physical being whose physicality I do not own, but which I must carry; that I must carry, but that I cannot see.

Back home I snuck peeks in the mirror as if I could own my body with my eyes. I was soon caught. The first time, I was young and it was a Thursday. Each Thursday was Dinner with Friends night. We warmed our evening nutritional shakes and sat in a tight ellipsis. We paced together, interspersing sips with conversation, so as to easily pace one's shake consumption with the rest of the group. **This was essential to group psychosocial harmony and cohesion. We must all be able to see each Citizen's full face.**

Fractionalization was forbidden. Sight of the full face was necessary to accurate recording. Citizens were Citizens because they were whole.

That one night, we were about to take our inaugural sips of the evening shake. We had our shakes at six, twelve, and six again. Our eyes held hands with each other. At precisely 6:00, we sat around the table, about to tilt our glasses backward. Then, my mother held up her hand.

"A record. Hold up, everyone."

She smiled hungrily and checked her device. I had looked in the mirror earlier that day, she quickly learned. I was compelled by a force I couldn't name to look at myself, again and again and again, a skipping-screen. I watched in horror as a figure identified as me stood there before the mirror, separating my meaningful body-glances with slow winks of each eye in turn. I wanted to close my eye around myself, just for a moment, to determine for myself what I could see. I wanted to do the taboo thing because I was still able, because, if nothing else, I could still blink. I had been **STOP-thinking** all day long, not making any sudden movements, and some animal part of me needed this one thing to be my own.

And it wasn't my own, not now: it belonged to the friends and to RSCH. The mirror swallowed me and spat me into someone else. Now the guests at my home had seen the mirror's account of my deviation, and RSCH, having learned of my actions via the contacts, also had it filed away. My whole body was cold. My mother played the recording again and again. I twisted and turned and blinked and repeated, and everyone watched in fascinated contempt.

When it ended, the screen went blank before sinking into the scenery. All eyes were on the real me, then, and my once-cold body was drowning in heat.

"You know what this means." My mother turned to me, holding up one finger in a pause. From the cabinet she retrieved a block of something; brown and sickly-smelling, whose fluids pooled limply beneath it. A slice, whose purpose was grounding. This was a consequence whose weight cannot be overstated.

I was expected to complete my shake at the same time as the others, lest I be written up by someone and sent to be treated. But I was also to finish the brown, oozing chunk; impossible without rushing down my shake. Everyone else began to drink and play table games so as to keep our respective minds sharp. We usually limited brain-training to school and then later to the applications installed on our contacts, but these weekly dinners ensured a degree of interpersonal training we would not otherwise receive.[3] Each guest left one eye lazily upon me and my cup and plate, the other on whomever sat beside them.

The slice began its grounding function, and I felt my heels sink deep into the floor, my legs slackening, hunks of flesh dripping toward the ground. I expanded outward, bulbous and straining against my garment. Everyone was now turned away from me, meanwhile I was expanding and melting at the same time. There was nothing else I could think about, the whole weight of my body pressed down on my skull. Everyone around me seemed to talk themselves right out of bodies, up through the tops of their head. They were engrossed in talk, whereas I was trapped in the flesh, gaining the mark of punishment.

Still they all spoke as if nothing was the matter, and nothing was the matter. At the end of the meal, several people recorded an image of us all sitting together. They would post them on the Network, and when everyone else around the Community had finished they would all scroll through and see who had gone to whose home. They would see me, partially-obscured but still grotesque. Despite distaste for the mirror, capturing images for the Network was a near-compulsory practice.

The volume in the room crept up as our guests began to leave. We engaged in all the goodbying. A woman entirely unrelated to me passed by on her way out the door as I remained seated in front of my empty dishware. She whispered, "The mirror always lies. And you too, you little animal."

The climate had killed all the animals like everything else outside as we retreated to communities. Animal was another word for deviant, sort of, because deviants no longer existed either.

Years after I escaped home, I put up with weeks, months, years of hunger just to avoid the supplements. I learned in the wild that RSCH lied when they said the shakes were our only option, when they claimed the other sources of food were gone. While the use of the term "food" was almost exclusively restricted to history classes, remembering us back to when each of us was a gambler, filling too much or too little, ever-incompletely nourished. Incomplete as it was, many non-shake, non-slice items were edible, even tasty. Ferns, mushrooms, soft grasses standing as tall as my knees. The vegetation had been let go in order to form a clear line of demarcation, one

---

3 This was also a way to detect early evidence of anti-or-asocial behavior.

that did not need to be reinforced with force, but one for which the specter of its crossing was a threat in and of itself.

WHAT UNAUTHORIZED   DID YOU PLACE ON YOUR TONGUE
DO YOU DARE USE THAT   TONGUE TO SPEAK

That night I went to bed too full. The following morning I would be measured at school, and be just slightly heavier than my designated range. By the design of the slice, to deviant me to indicate my deviance. I would be monitored at lunch that day. Although not explicit, the public shame incurred by such supervision, such quarantine from the group, such whispered questions from teachers and nurses, all of it was as punishing as the putrid slice itself, which hung in me like a magnet to attract its ilk. The feeding; the ache in my stomach, the wideness, the disobedience write-up for said wideness, the report home, did you

know is   and compared to the normalcy charts this is simply   outlandish disgusting

That was the day I first met Reya. Back then, I didn't know their Reya, so I called them the name they wore in school, untrue as the faux-Citizen legs they used to blend. In my face that day they swear they saw it all: our woods, our us, our abandoning everything like names and legs and Citizenship. Maybe it was my forced quarantine, presuming this deviation to be intentional rather than fallen-into.

After that day's class, they pulled me into a dark place near the school building. This place had no NewGrass, and made my vision—my contacts—fuzz and blot. They held my ear to their lips, which brushed my lobes as they whispered. This in itself was flirting with danger. I felt a shiver reach each notch of my back in turn.

> *"They are going to re-measure you this afternoon they will say they want you to go free & they want you*
> *to be good but your body was a failure and it was a shame*
> *because they want to protect their own. This is a lie. You can make*
> *yourself again."*

When we were through, the spot vanished, my vision cleared, and Reya was, for a moment, gone, too. They returned the next day as if nothing had happened. But it had, I was sure, and it was the first sure I had felt beyond RSCH. The first time I felt the axe—though it was not an axe, but a notion—graze my neck.

I am taking my time because there is much to remember, and I do not want to turn blue with the forgetting.

KNOW THIS

there is no [purity]
just power; its
beneficiaries &
our collective dis ease

artificial salvation: you are
violence in its making, metal
and bone awaiting break
iron to be wrought, blue before
its red. you're bright shining
oil in the sunlight.

the moment they fix you they give you a new   number, a new name and they
do not ask   what you are called nor are you expected   to remember.
although you are not living   real life they say, welcome   to health and
to purity   !   they moan   healthily,   allow
us 2 fix   (make)   just   this little bit and you   will
finally   be free.

where does freedom turn   when a body not my own
yet never a friend   none of mine   shall   i
turn the fire in   my belly to water or deny it   oxygen; ashes to be scraped
from its   heart///h

Periodically RSCH sends its RSCH to clip the trees that give us air. It has always been known that this is also a hunt for the deviants hiding out, not to axe but to scout. Each time they did this I felt smaller and bigger at once: less ability to move, little to cover me. I couldn't extend to the edges of myself for fear of being seen. Pruned. Outside was a dark vacuum of carbon dioxide. The trees protect the everyone but the no one most of all.

Back in the mirror days, it felt as though I would last forever as an image of an image of myself. It took a nude video of me staring into it, checking, checking, checking again the moment my eyes left it, as though something sick and demented lived on its other side waiting to twist my body to its desires the moment my eyes left the glass. The video was attached to my name and posted to the Network.

For a long period after that, no one but Reya spoke to me. Who would want to catch what I had? For several Community dinners after it occurred I had watch it in my AR contacts to remind me of the consequences of my disobedience. All would relish watching that memory me sip the shake, and then look in the mirror, and then be fast-forwarded to the shake, and grow bulbous, and again, and again, and all of them became RSCH for a moment, and this was their source of pleasure, this was their true aliment; I was being eaten alive, eaten in and by silence.

At first, in the thick, anxious silence of the trees, I had cried to Reya in anger, swung my hands uselessly in misplaced aggression, occasionally placing a meaningless hit on Reya's bruised body.

"You can't make them grow," Reya would laugh. They were a head taller than me, and my swings mostly hit their chest. "Only the supplements can do that."

"I don't care about supplements," I would say, though I cared very much. "I want to go back."

"They wouldn't let you if you tried."

"You did. With your fake legs."

"They have you on video," Reya said, with a patience that hurt. "It's all over the Network. You made your bed."

Another oldworld phrase they must have learned in the wild. Like the rest of the bodies out here, we slept in brushpiles, under cover of tall trees and low shrubs.

"It means that you chose this," Reya said, pointing with one crutch to our pushed-together piles.

My last day in school was alone. No Reya. My measurements that day said **out of proportion**. My mother blithely attributed this to the slices I had had to consume, punishment for my latest recorded infraction

> small deviances committed by children and adolescents which challenge the wholeness of the individual, and thus, the collective body. Networked (re)presentation of said infractions served once again to unite the Community.

the carving of my thighs with slice-knives and refusal of the shakes. I could not be seen like this. **You can not be seen like this.** I agreed, proceeded down the questionnaire required of each infracting child before conditional pardon was granted.

Q: What does RSCH stand for?

A: The advancement and ascension of the Pureself to its deserved place as master of its body.

Q: Is RSCH happening here?

A: Yes.

Q: What makes a deviant?

A: An essence that offends.

Q: What are we running from?

A: We are walking.

Q: What is RSCH?

A: A making of Truth.

you take me by the

memory. it is all you know
i am. taken by the memory
hung by the treebranch
before any dream bore
fruits

RSCH kept with tradition, making us in twos. Male and female. This was done to teach us a lifestyle of compliance and orderliness, and a means by which to live it even before we were old enough to understand. Girls answered to "she" and "her," boys to "he" and "him." There was no reason for it, for the use of these words and not others. We did not need sex the way the animals we were used to, back when we were truly no more than bodies made by unrighteous accident. Now we were clean and our parts were principle. They were words unto themselves. The breasts said girl. The opening said girl. They had no use but to speak the word for what I was. To remember the order inside and around me. For boys, the same. The genders were educational purposes, and frequently cited in lessons on acceptance for what we cannot and should not change, trust the RSCH process, its ever-movement toward enlightenment, evermore to progress.

And before transcending the body there was perfecting the body, which to RSCH came in two styles, each with its distinct measurements, parts, and functions. This was the way things were, the natural way. There were no anomalies, except when there were, and they were born-deviant and secreted away, but they did not exist: not Citizens and never having been, their bodies were at once entrapped and nonexistent.

It was not until someone spoke the possibility allowed

allowed   aloud that I was able to think it.

I will never forget that day that I first had words — or words for the left-absence — of unthinkable bodies.

It began like this. "What happens," a classmate asked, "when you don't have either one?" Then we turned to stare at him. We all did, as if moved by one singular force at once. His eyes were wide. Pale green. He shook at our stares. His eyes were trained on some unfixed spot at the front of the classroom, not on anything of import. We all held our breath.

Each of our teachers wore knee-length garments with white translucent tights. Their shoes made no sound against the floor, having been manufactured to allow silent movement, making it easier to catch and stymie bad behavior. Though educators were not RSCH, they were a half-step above the rest of us, having been tapped as teenagers to train directly under RSCH.

And why do you ask? asked the teacher in her most chilling RSCH tone, all bold with hard-lines, thick-shaped and pasty. She grew taller, bigger, more foreboding, even as she remained the same as always. It was as if a spotlight had been cast upon the boy and his wild, wide green eyes. Reya was in the classroom, too, but I did not yet know what to look for.

I believe, our teacher continued, **this to be a teachable moment. To have neither is to be illegal. That is, to not be.**

Silence.

Do you know anyone like this? She stood over him. A gardener prepared to snip a weed, back hunched and still towering, at least in effect.

Looking back were his bright green eyes. Greener than NewGrass.

Stand up. She could not press the tips of her fingers into his shoulders, but could use the nails, which were long, rounded semi-circles with purple underbeds. Her living skin did not so much as brush him, only those immaculate nails. And there he was: green-eyed boy in the center of the room. He was so pale, always but especially now; it looked as though his blood had turned to bone. Looking away from the boy (we don't recall his name; he has none now, he's not and gone.) I spotted a body, Reya's, tensing quietly, and then releasing, with such subtlety I questioned my own eyes.

Do you have your documents, said the teacher. It was not a question.

Green-eyes did not answer immediately. I fingered the hem of my jumpsuit. My documentation was printed onto my undergarments. Many of us had taken to doing this after a spate of reports came out involving RSCH asking Citizens for their documents in secondary, non-digital forms. As a reason, they cited the increasing number of hackers attempting to override the documents of demoted Citizens, **so as to allow intra-Community breakdown.**

No? Off with your clothes, then. She also expected to see his documents underneath. Text appeared on the HoloScreen in the center of the room.

IF YOU DO NOT MAKE AVAILABLE YOUR DOCUMENTS YOU WILL MAKE AVAILABLE YOUR B

The "**ODY**" glitched. It lagged behind the "**B**."

We were not permitted to see fellow Citizens' bodies bare, although we discussed the workings of the body in its glorious, Pure totality near everyday. All of us looked around, panicked, waiting for someone to tell us whether or not we were supposed to look. A look away was a refusal to see reality, to see guilt. But looking too intently suggested illegitimate interest in and even desire for the body. Some place must exist in between those two, but it seemed that the location of that safe middle-ground was ever-shifting.

So we just kept looking. This was something we needed to see. Green-eyes unbuttoned his jumpsuit. We saw. It's a blackened gash in the mind. Several police emerged from nowhere, where they always were. Among them was a man in gloves, who took Green-eyes's blood in a small vial. They made a great show of shuffling him to the medical center.

Our teacher stood facing the door of the classroom, following the procession with her eyes, most likely recording the scene.

"I hope he decides to get better," she said.

She said I said in me. My head.

I am watching the memory from outside my mind. I feel something looking over the shoulder of my psyche. I cannot stop it. I attempt to **STOPTHOUGHT** but the muck rushes through in long torrents.

This morning I stared down at my two born-hands and born-arms and felt a rising hostility I had never felt before. I feel worry. I feel fear. I am living in the present but I can hardly see it. I hardly have any movement left in me. I can't tell   where I am   yet but I can say

5. Words are the current   the currency.

The most powerful thing about RSCH is its words. The worlds it deals. Deviant, irresponsible, dangerous—handing them to us like the old pharmacist would with pills, small capsules of cure, before those pill-needing ailments were cured for good

through several waves of eliminations, in which proto-RSCH incentivized parents of defective children to give them up in exchange for a high Network rating. These waves proved insufficient to root out the deviants, who continued to be born. Soon after, RSCH banned all skin-to-skin contact between human beings who had reached pubescence, and harvested embryos exclusively in their laboratories, assigning each of them to worthy guardians who had already completed the requisite psychological testing.

Now, all skin-skin contact was banned as a matter of safety.

And so words become the current and currency. They change the way the body looks. They are more powerful than all the hormone supplements ever made and packed together tighter in bodies than shots in crates.

What alchemy is it that makes word become world. That turns permission into compensation, that turns a name into a something, that gives a name its teeth.

What was cure, anyway? Did the Recitizened Citizen come back unrecognizable? Did cure turn beautiful, shine with pleasure? Was the word of cure itself the value in it? Was this the reason why a different CLASS of Citizen took on a different cast, as if the shadow, the shadow of wrong, had been wiped clean by curative tonic?

Nothing changed, it all did. In the shadow of the real I have hardly a crawlspace to think these things. I think them in gaps and in waves, in gaps where my thoughts break with RSCH, in the tiny openings wherein connections fray, blank. I am losing the rest of me. But I think or dream   into the breaks.

Where am I now. I have no words to tell, only that it's blue here, every shade of it but no other. It can only be said in a sound that hasn't yet been made, and that if made is unrecordable because it would not be RSCH-permitted. I think there are more things here than blue but only blue I can grasp. And what is due but the color I am told it is. What is blue. I'm thinking of the green-eyed boy again. Of my eyes, brown. The tiny pieces of colors that appear to be green at their very edges, forbidden greens, because my eyes are wholly brown and so they are in Truth.

Blue, drowning now. I feel large.

Education had long been mandatory in the Community. Educe means *to lead out*, and **to educate (therefore) is to bring forth the inborn abilities of the Pure body and mind, to attempt to synchronize the body and mind; to allow the mind to discipline the body to its fullest extent**.

Our educators wandered the halls and the classrooms in order to lead out the Citizen within us all. By lines we were led around the school's grounds, to the restrooms and back, to eat and back to class. At school we walked only on the turf and never on the NewGrass, and because we remained in line the NewGrass remained green and lush. The lines were organized by sex. One accidental line-crossing infraction led to a warning, unless it was combined with real or perceived appearance-modification that suggested physiological confusion. Two would result in immediate referral to the nurse and most likely a stint outside school, with RSCH. I had not considered any of this strange until Reya remarked on it to me, sighing their strange relief at not having been educated in the time of initial line-making.

"Funny, isn't it? That we need documents to prove something that's meant to be natural." Reya had said this between gasps beneath their labored breath. They had run here from the forming lines, and I had followed by accident or some other unnameable force. We were in a patch behind the school and it was twilight. It was nowhere and no one   could see us.

I said, "Isn't it funny," repeating them, believing in my repetition to be making sense of our shared spontaneous flight.

Silence. I said again, "Isn't it…I guess I hadn't…"

Reya placed a cool hand over my mouth. I had never felt anyone's hand on me before, none but RSCH, whose hands were not hands but gloves which left my bodily purity intact. Their hand smelled like something I'd later call soil. At the time, it smelled deviant, as did all things with detectable odors.

They removed their hand, saying, "it's not funny, really. It's funny… only in the way things are when you're trying to swallow them but then you realize—" Their hand flew to their clavicle and their eyes emptied, "—that it's stuck in your throat." I noticed Reya's clavicle, the way the bone stuck bluntly through their skin, slightly pinker than my own.

It was an unauthorized use of the word. *Funny.* I felt uncomfortable.

Unsure of what was stuck in their throat, I thought back to Reya's tense body and the time of the green-eyed boy, then fresh in my memory. I looked Reya up and down again, thinking something unthinkable. As if hearing me, they leaned closer, themself attempting to educe, induce, something in me I had long since been led out of.

Finally I spoke unthinking. "Did your body do something to you. Back there. When they were talking to him." I thought I had had the will to use a question mark, but perhaps I, too, was a timid little   little

Reya's eyes narrowed. They spat on me. The spittle fanned and split and fanned and split and I felt as though every inch of my skin had been touched by a great, sweating rag. I stifled a scream and made to wipe it, although I realized quickly I had nothing to wipe with that would not also be contaminated.

"My body didn't do anything to me," they said. "That shaking was all me. I did it with my whole being. It was all me."

"It's a thing your body does. Your mind is the thing that can, well— you know, it can regulate, discipline."

"You say that as if you didn't just scream without thinking about it." They looked me near the eye, concerned that the contacts I at the time had installed (but whose functions, I would learn, didn't exist in nowhere) would somehow reactivate if we acknowledged each other fully, if we pinned ourselves in space and time.

"That green-eyed kid isn't going to come back. And don't you scream at my spit as if you aren't already a little deviant." Which interpretation of Reya's ambiguous phrasing was worse? The worst was really the ambiguity itself, which RSCH eliminated in all cases.[4]

A little deviant. A little...little. I remembered the way my body looked in the mirror, the way those moments played again and again in the minds of our former guests—many of whom would, no doubt, return again later in the hopes of another spectacle. I watched Reya's lips, pointedly avoided their eyes. Their lips. Slick with spit. My mouth recalled their hand, soiled.

---

4 The truth is already here, it is either known or yet-known.

Annually, we signed a student-educator contract.

"When you sign the contract," a teacher might say, "you are bound by it."

We could not be educated unless we signed it.

Schooling was mandatory. Truants, in their truancy, renounced Citizenship status.

At the collection of the contracts we were told: "Remember that you have chosen to obey these guidelines."

Each school contained several subjects   all taught daily at predictable times whose precise details only teachers could access. Classrooms held no clocks.

We learned to meet age-bracketed social and psychological goals. With age we took on more courses regarding moral and social responsibility. Instruction, which took place face-to-face, was supplemented by a log of the same information, which was aggregated to our contacts' respective hard-drives. We continued our studies at home, reviewing imported information and practicing requisite social skills. The school building itself was not necessary to educe us, but evidence-based research suggested its utility, and the utility of the in-person classroom, toward maintaining compliance. In-person instruction also allowed a personalization of consequences for those who strayed off-task: we consumed visual input from the HoloScreen at the head of each classroom, which tracked each pupil   and   registered aberrant unfocus, among other things forbidden in our contract.

Reya and the green-eyed boy shared something in common—their bodies each had grown in a way RSCH did not like. To RSCH this was a personal offense: a blow to their creative power and scientific knowledge. They were whittled, buried, downed to a fine and invisible point—but a tiny poking point all the same.

Reya, born differently-embodied than RSCH predicted, poked enough to draw blood. It was a revelation of RSCH's weakness, this *possibility* that could not be overcome. *Chance* was still a wrench. It begged the question: could a body be salvageable when it had not yet had time to choose deviance but instead was simply cursed with it? How was it that deviance was both an unchanging biological truth *and* a pathogen to be excommunicated? In time, Reya had been able to ask me all of these things, though in much more personal and complicated terms. RSCH asked none of it in words but did it away in whittling.

As a born-deviant, Reya was recipient of RSCH authority stripped to its most naked and distilled form. They attributed their extensive knowledge and powerful, early speculation on its machinations to this exposure, to this nudity before power which was itself naked. Their home had been full of tech installed at the time of their birth, while they were kept at RSCH for monitoring. One day, their parents had returned home from data-working and found it there, all those blinking blue lights giving way to a hall of HoloScreens, all functioning as mirrors through which Reya was not allowed to look and dotted by buttons Reya was not allowed to touch.

The buttons alerted RSCH to the times Reya needed help. At a parent's press, any installed button would send RSCH help home. Sometimes Reya went somewhere else to get it, other times, help was administered on their hall or bedroom floor.

Reya's parents weren't immune from RSCH suspicion. Sometimes their faces leaked into frowns and then, just in time, turned into smiles. Once they exceeded their allotted period in the state of despair (which they were generously granted in Reya's infancy), they had had to move on to the state of acceptance, taking private Citizenship and comportment courses. They kept journals, which RSCH would check the against their biometric data, tracking potential noncompliance in those whose bodily fluids had produced one so defective. Together with weekly visits from RSCH workers, highly-frequent checkups for Reya and their parents, this self-maintenance completed

RSCH's holistic approach to improvement.

"It's inevitable they're going to see me do something wrong," Reya told me. They often spoke in | tenses violating reason, violating order, confusing past and present and they

(They. As long as I'm many, they can't catch all of me, they said of the pronoun, whose usage—if brought up in the Community— would have them sent immediately for RSCH assessment.)

and I and one and many.

They told me: "I was walking down the street back when I thought I could still look safe. Back when I believed I passed for something. I suddenly felt this blinding shot of pain inside my chest and I felt I was collapsing in every way but body. Next thing I knew, I was in a room that looked windowless and wallless and lawless and two faceless   RSCH were—my clothes, I don't know where they went. RSCH were there. I was horizontal. I felt a tap and I knew they were taking blood, but also all that data, taking out that chip and putting it on their screen. They all but read my mind, you know?"   I know

I knew. I know

"And I was out as soon as I realized that. Back on the street as though nothing had happened, not even dizzy, although I'm positive they took blood from me. Near-positive? I searched all the channels back then, when I thought they could still provide useful information to me and I found nothing about these weird wall-less rooms and missing time. I couldn't try to track it. My head would try to burst when I did."

"And then you started living away from everything."

"Yeah, it was either that or..." Reya could never bring themself to say *kidnapped*; *taken*. There were some words that were too against the Truth and at the same time too true to be spoken, all these things we are not ready to face in their strange and doubled state.

"I had already started eating some of the stuff in the woods. Sneaking off, smelling scary. Maybe it was part of their plan, to let me do that. Maybe they're still watching now, who knows." After sitting in their memories and telling me these stories for too long, Reya began to speak like this, in short, humorless exclamations. Random disjointed phrases, lots of. Stops. "Once you start foraging—that's the word for digging stuff up out of the ground to eat. Your body realizes it can't take the supplement. It just can't. At least, my wrong body can't. My body..." And they wouldn't finish the sentence, they would be overcome by awe and rage and confusion, and I'd wish I could feel that many things about my body at once, rather than searing, jarring, skin-lifting hatred. Hatred that made me deviant and deviate. Hatred that marked me Uncitizen myself. Hatred whose reason and whose consequence existed on the same side of some unknowable line up behind me, keeping me   keeping me.

Reya's parents grew increasingly enthusiastic about compliance when Reya came back from this mysterious place, although because the place Reya went to does not exist, Reya had in truth never left. Indeed there had been a Reya like a ghost in the house while they were at the unplace where all the unthings happened or did not happen, attached to the walls and floorboards their parents couldn't wash. Reya was sure of this. At the time, Reya was not known as Reya, but by a number—seventy-seven—and before that by some name to which they no longer have access—either way, in the mysterious place Reya was seventy-seven and at home remained the Reya by an older name.

Their legs were gone when they got out of the place that was no place. "I assume for practical reasons." Segments of their memory, too: overwritten, washed, redone, blued-up, dimmed, honed, heightened, tightened, loose.

I was made
with several defects
in mind. First:
the memory

All of the surgeries occurred under the cover of darkness, where the stability of reality itself could only be hoped for, maybe anticipated, but never assured. This was vital: if the surgeries were real and true they would be done. But under the cover of darkness I learned that sometimes pain was so delicious that RSCH, of course, would have had to bar us from it. I learned that the word *pleasure* had once been a desired-thing, and thus that words could change in meaning. That the truth was

4 3 8 5 7 3 8 7 4 - 9 2 4 7 6 6 & 7 & 7 5 _ _ - 4 # 3 # 5 - _ - 98874472819#ˆ6*(((9*****0)__9

WAS   S PAIN

tasted like power, like *becoming*. Pain tasted like I could do something other than *have been*; that an active *me* was possible, that tenses existed for reason more than demarcating before, falsehood, darkness and today, light, truth. I could, for example, make my own pain. I did this occasionally in ways I was not proud of. I spent even more time anticipating the pain I would at some point make myself: burying action in possible until I had no space, drawing blood from that overfull future. I realized (if) I must hurt, let me determine which area will meet the next blow.

RSCH couldn't cause pain, too   but they could
not, it was impossible, because it was   help   beneficent

and beneficent
only, to the Community populace.

In between the pain I was better able to think. I wondered what they were, RSCH, when the other letters were still there. When we could pronounce their name without sore throats. RSCH had been four letters as long as I had known it, unpronounceable without those vowels long gone, as if it would not exist but for those things that lurked in its shadow.

I wondered why, when the hormones first came, my stomach knew to twist, my mind revolting at the foreign substance as if I were a Citizen still. When the needle met my skin, I squealed. My blood rushed to a silent point, liquid languiding my thigh. I could see its sickening movement just beneath my skin. It was in me, it was in me, and I was and would forever be tainted.

After a time, Reya had jerked my arm from its sad dangling location: "Don't you feel strong? Don't you feel like they are holding you a little less tightly now? How does it feel to defy them for the first time?" How did they *think* it felt?

I knew I felt hot, tired, and soggy.

Then, their anger: "You got all of this by choice and now you're just—just— !"

(And on and on, this was our game: my ungrateful freedom and their condemnation.)

"Just because you're deciding when to hurt and how you hurt doesn't mean you're doing something brave or special," said Reya once. We were eating some mushrooms from the ground then. I had had some but not all of the surgeries I sought. Between mushrooms we'd sip carafes of non-potable water, whose effects our bodies, already poison|ed, nullified.

"I'm not special," I said. "I just hate this..." I pinched a pocket of skin between my index and thumbnails until a shallow well of blood emerged. I licked the blood from my fingers before resuming a mushroom. "...This, this, *thing*. So it's all got to go somehow."

Reya stood and came right up close to me. There was hardly space between the feet of their crutches and my crossed legs, and I could almost feel Reya's breath on my hair.

"Don't you see you're still giving them what they want?" Reya demanded. "Giving them a body you think is deviant, changing it, trying to get a result you think is Pure?"

I must have had the second stomach installed when they asked, because I remember reaching down and clasping it, feeling through the sticky-slick flesh the mushrooms inside. Between the second stomach — a holding space for spare food I would prefer to give back to the ground — and my body is a great curve of negative space.

"Just call them RSCH," I replied, "'Them' sounds so... *hostile*." I didn't know why I said this. I brought my left fist to my right cheekbone, hearing a thud from within my own head.

"You're *right*, I'm hostile. What, did they tell you to do that, too?" Reya gestured at my face. I would have a bruise soon. Upset blood.

"And no, I won't call them that stupid, excavated word, whatever. With its guts blown out. Washed and Pure and so clean it's see-through... that's where they hide. I want to know the rest." Reya slammed their own fist against the tree behind our backs. Their arms were large, hard, sleek with muscle from the constant work of crutching their entire body's weight. Unlike the rest of Reya's body, their arms were scarless.

They continued: "I'm not going to make them real. They need us to do this to be real and I'm so tired. What if we all just one day pretended they didn't exist?"

"Well, if we were all *pretending*, we'd be..."

"I mean, what if we... no. As soon as I say it, it's gone. I think it's a... something in there blanks me," they cocked their head to one side and I knew they meant that thing in their neck, buried too deep and secure even for the Operator to take, bound by materials unknown to any of us, this singular and paradigmatic reminder of RSCH's shadow. It played its constant memory games with Reya, compelling them to view their data at random moments and then suddenly erasing it all. Reya called this *feasting famine*, after an archaic phrase. They said it was what happened when RSCH got our data, all our memories RSCH stock. Their stock was the feast. We, our stocks, were fed and famished.

&in the whitenight wake of running
kiss the river mouth
kiss the differance
make the body
tenderly
of meat and knot

dark-rose creamwhite hue
elsewhere spaces in their
lipful texture
scathed   beat remember
as if made
the scar, waking

stripped all bodies
like sand like salt like
fear a garnish be
-tween bones and meat.

some can't cry it all out.
some may be washed;
others watched. all one
amassing grief like water
eats a cliff.

In this record I do a lot of train-thinking, curving the story I'm giving in unwieldy ways. If it is being consumed now, the consumer should know they are winding, they are going someplace with me that has not yet been revealed. I don't know myself where this is going. This is the deviance, the danger. How to deviate when one's course is not yet made up? Be the body intervening someone else's. Move as a mix-up.

I can't ruminate too long on my circumstances or else I'll blank entirely. I can't aware of where I am because it makes the time slip faster.

I should be (within) a space of mindfulness, a space to allow RSCH to take thoughtflight in the mind, for the truth to sow itself. Rumination leads to anxiety, leads to disorder, leads to the uncontained publics **that led us, in the past, to our downfall**. Overthinking will be the death of all that is good and Pure, every stray marking the blank white surface of the clean-sound mine with a great dark stain the shade of the forest. With the contacts our minds are tracked, thoughts whose wondering wandering ma lingering is unsatisfactory are spottable, correctable, usually before it is too late.

And then there is this record, this public record I am making with my all in my head. All my life is. There are no words for this that I know, so I make them with my pondering, my back-and-forth movement.

I am trying not to be afraid. I am trying not to think about windows. The light doesn't reach us directly anymore, ever. When we believed in our bodies enough to bare bear them to the sun, we were burnt, we were suffocated, we crumpled beneath the weight of our own excess. And the excess was eliminated. RSCH made became designed the Community, its spherical protective surface whose beginning and end are unknown to all of us.

RSCH emerged amidst social chaos. They battled enemies with monstrous, deviant bodies and, armed with the objective truth, won. They built a space to protect us and ultimately to free us; to provide us a space to manage ourselves into transcendence of the body entirely. Through early periods of experimentation, RSCH found the best practices for curbing deviance, perfecting the art of governance. They sealed the windows. A Citizen had only to be compliant, to be health-promoting. Safety was the deviance so far away it almost, though not quite, vanished behind the horizon.

For the horizon there was RSCH to think   thank.   Before RSCH there was no old and new, but the juncture and hatch between. They split Pure and Impure like hair between comb with the language of a dense codex the rest would never see, a manual of deviancies so vast and complete only a dr could read it. Yet deviance and RSCH, hungry, remained, wording dispose of their hunger. The newest word was MA, "misplaced aggression," presenting comorbid with almost all other forms of deviance. The average Uncitizen, upon being Uncitizened, would be by default given the mark.

> I'm MA now, I'm sure. I don't know for sure because I haven't
> heard so from RSCH. I haven't caught up with myself since a
> while   surveying things I already trying up to the
> surface

Diagnoses, including MA, were RSCH's first and more effective line of defense against deviance. Met with a description, the foe becomes knowable, that is, conquerable, that is, purifiable. One day there would be enough words to Know the entire body, and then, only then, would we reach enlightenment.

We, not me. We worked toward enlightenment while the rest do the dirty work. Lay blue in the forest pumped up with the dregs of the fat of the drip of the bodies crowing out their skins.

> I'm doing the dirty work, self.
> Get a grip. I'm laying, prone
> in here. Everything's blue, and I'm sick
> of seeing saying soaking in
> it. I'm sick of remembering not seeing
> Reya
> Yes, I am SICK I am SICK I am SICK and as a SICK I carry the

SICK of every other to ever SICK and around me   to PROGRESS like   a SICK   CARRY SICK   like a KNOWN

I CARRY HUMANITY IN MY POCKET AND YOU R

EPAY ME WITH WHAT

6. This is the beginning of the story.

I am in a waiting room.
About to be called
A string of numbers I do not recognize.
This is where the story starts. I'm frozen.
here

    I am trying to walk back into it backward, place myself outside
RSCH thought. I am in a space where things happen in orders
that don't make sense, where life is allowed to be senseless
to sense the rest of it.

    So I impurify my grammar. Mix tenses. Be unpleasant,
as I must be

    something.

Deep in RSCH and outside the law. In the law but without it.

Nothing in particular to describe. It is all white in here, so white I forget I can see at all, forget the backs of my eyelids haven't simply turned white and I am seeing them only, forget there isn't some finger holding my eyes shut. In truth there is simply no place for eye   to rest. There are no windows. There is no light. Blank walls keep me inside, so nothing I felt to look at them is not to look at all. I cannot see them so the walls are not there and yet the walls must be there to protect me from what I cannot see.

I know I'm standing.

Although this room is as dry and bare, I'm drowning.

I'm drowning many times: in bewilderment, in impossible. In this place where I was and where wasn't real.

There was no door (I am back to my tense). It feels felt as though I just saw its rectangular edict fade quick into the wall so that the door through which I entered was never. I was confused as to how I got in. A window grew in its place though I could not access it. I felt we were far above ground.

Although there was no door, I sensed that if the need arose, one would manifest.

All this was emptiness because there was no time to keep. If it was kept by someone, it passed, and I grew empty.

There was no emptiness like this one. I was so empty I forgot hunger. I forgot the difference between hungry and alone. I forgot to think of keeping time; I had nowhere to put it. I thought riddles and thought I saw them moving in the shadows of the black. I considered the clock and the empty inexplicable left in between. I thought about numbers as bodies and wondered my number in the lineage.

Reya once told me that when you're off to a place you don't know, never eat the food. Just after they said it, their face turned startled, and they continued, "And don't take this too seriously, okay?"

But I knew it was true. I was already afraid to offset the tender gravitational balance. Of course I wouldn't eat. I had enough inside me.

> I am seated at a makeshift table. It is too clean for me to touch. In front of me is a shake that looks like all the others ever looked. It sits inside an unmarked bottle. If looked at from a certain angle, the bottle can blend seamlessly with the table itself.

> I am not still in the waiting room but I am (a) waiting room. Awaiting room   in this stomach so full of lonely. A forbidden feeling.

> This place I am feels different from the clinic. It is dark like the inside of an organ. There is nothing to see except for the table and shake. I cannot see my body. I can sense the space around me only. I can feel other eyes on me. I can fear other eyes on me. I am staring down the shake and re-membering my mother. Her long arms make ribbons.

"Something I didn't understand until I met you is why they want us to eat together so much," Reya had continued, back in the early days. "Like, *dinner with friends?*" I knew the bit about the extra cameras, the extra angles—with all those *friends* around the table, they got more data. More memory. More images, and stuff.

"But...it just seems so strange to me. Put everyone in houses, make them go to different peoples' all the time. Say the family is the fundamental unit that must, at given times, be expanded. It doesn't make sense."

"They make sense," I reminded them.

"They make us." *They make nonsense.*

"No, they named us as the things we already are."

"Do you really believe you were a Citizen back then? That when they made sense they made the person who ended up here?"

> Shake in my mouth. Memories in my eyes. Body big by the moment. Mud in my throat. My garments, gone, I burst into my nakedness as if I chose it. My hand the size of trees. My sweat the pore like rain. I am bigger than my own shadow.

EXCERPT
THE PURITY COMMISSION: YEARLY REPORT
[CONVERSATION BETWEEN DR. 3238 & DR. 10390]

3238: Axe as normal, subject grounded. What's the hold-up in getting her lifted?

10390: Arial scan, but it won't be long now. Police have been issued to the wilds' perimeter. 77 sighted alongside subject.

3238: Captured?

10390: Not this one. Its anatomy is severely unrecognizable. Unchipped, untagged—some grotesque attempt at medicine left the piece but removed its function.

[...]

3238: Transfer has been completed. Subject failed to comply with voluntary offer.   administration beginning promptly.

Hands on my arms, mouth wide open. In the forest I remember a girl with a stitched mouth, her choice to speak Impurely, only through her hands. I feel two large hands, one on each arm, and I realize I am being touched by a stranger. I am still   heavy, and someone is bending over me. I stare into a dreamscape above and see faces looking at my own, each tinted teal and swimming as if covered by the past's Pure water. I drift gradually away from the faces, realize I am walking.

I was walking in the woods I knew, on the path to get the hormones. I needed to stop. I tried to say no but it came out as sludge. I stopped my legs but my dreamlegs kept walking. I stopped my dreamlegs and my dreambody forced me to crawl. No, no, no directions here. I remembered myself into a shroud of darkness, the path in front of and behind me a mystery: my legs could move in any direction and not reveal the way. The lights came on. I was half in the dreamspace, half out, and here it was again. Teal. The bodies in the woods reached out of the soil to me, offering comfort. Hands again outstretched and the faces became faces or stones.

FALLERE_TEST_77

Subject reached complete infancy on   Was withheld from assigned family due to abnormality e.450 (sexual ambigui- ty type 4.2). The following was recorded on   w i t h assigned guardians (EN & DU).

3238: Before we begin, is there anything we might like to know about either of you?

EN: First of all, I would like to thank you and the rest of RSCH for the incredible work you all do each day to keep our Community safe and illuminated. And I want to thank you in particular for gestating our little boy.

3238: That's why we've brought you here. 77 is no boy. There is a fault.

DU: Wait, no! We've been tested. We've been checked. We were cleared as healthy—

3238: No interruptions, please. First warning for insubordina- tion. First warning for panic-induced behavior. You will relin- quish 77 so as to ensure its rehabilitation prior to returning to your home.

[MUFFLED]

3238: It is, and you know to trust us as our knowledge remains at the cutting-edge. If you were not to choose to submit 77 for test- ing, you both—and those genetically related to you both—would have to undergo periodic testing to ensure compliance.

EN: We will do anything we need to do to ensure a healthy future for all Citizens. We are a part of the national body and we must do what we can to paste the cracks. Our—ou—77, I mean, should be submitted for testing, however intense and lengthy such testing would be.

[SILENCE]

3238: Thank you for choosing to help us protect the safety and security of all. If you will follow us, outtake is right this way. After a brief procedure to ensure that this unfortunate situation will not occur again, you will be free to go.

[SILENCE]

[SHUFFLING]

3238: As you learned in school, our mission and purpose is to Supply Knowledge For The Protection of Reason and Bodily Wholeness and to Edify the Public on Living a Healthy Lifestyle (SKFTPRBWEPHL)

which state is the one
most desirable to you? that of cut cartilage
rancid outside
of mind space or both?
which allows entrance,
on one precondition: ill
unmake what was before

7. This is I, resurfaced.

I've been gone for a long time. This is i, resurfaced. I'm here outside of time but still bound by it. I can expect the shakes, the drs, the check-ups and -ins, all running on that internal schedule I will never know. Last time I could think I asked and was told to accept uncertainty. And then my body, back-first on a thin tray, was examined for concealed signs of disobedience.

I will insert what I can glean. Can't tell you what or who I'm writing on. I'm writing this for public record. I'm writing I'm writing so they won't forget me into

I am still sequestering my   thoughts.

There is an oldworld word called psychopathy. It is in history books alongside other words I have since forgotten   have been done to forget. I remember this one, though, and I remember its section-header: "early attempts at defining and disposing of the Noncitizen." There were words there in other englishes, too, I think, listed as artifacts for our consumption. Many more were buried forever beneath history, which I always imagine as weighing the sum of every device holding every element ever made, from chips into hard drives, from disks into books, from books, even, into tablets, to minerals, to trees, to bodies. Did RSCH find the stones from so far before even the oldworld that at the time, there was no world at all?

A dr walks in—white and sharp and glaring as his coat. He pushes into me some clear fluids, and I feel nauseated at the thought and sight of my now-rippling skin. I'm gagging now, spitting, spluttering—

"The covering will do," dr says. It's over. I wave my arms wildly while I still can, wiggle my legs until they go immobile beneath the cover's weight.

Gestures were considered vulgar, animalistic, far departed from the rational mind. Once there were people who could not hear and their englishes spoke in gestures, but they were reported to the authorities for their Inability to Vocalize, soon found to be co-morbid with MA

all deviancies, it seemed, corresponded to a heightened tendency toward aggression and overall uncivil response to RSCH intervention.

I can no longer move. I can make sounds, still, but no noise — RSCH cannot detect any disruption I attempt to make. The chips the drs have embedded below each ear

> which are not evidence of bodily desecration or self-hacking because RSCH cannot desecrate nor hack, only treat; in this case, they do not treat, because no drs are also ill
>
> one be both a dr and ill
>
> but enhance — drs are enhanceable through such means because they have already proven their good health.

immunize them to certain frequencies such as those the patients cry in.

I can no longer think of movement. I can think the word movement but no substance. Instead, I try to think about 77, about those initials, EN and DU, about all the meanings still beyond my reach, as if I could reach. Wonders fill the leaky spaces where I once spoke to my limbs.

A dr reads my blood pressure or heart rate, recording me numerically on an invisible screen   an invisible scream.

I, too, have a number, one far higher than 77, though I have no idea whether or not patient numbers grow chronologically; if they're anything like our given names, they are periodically recycled. A name lives and a name fades, then it is assigned anew. We went by our names to our neighbors and families and coworkers, and to drs and the police we were the numbers they called us. Once defected, the Citizenship identification number was promptly stripped from an Uncitizen. It was reassigned immediately; a returned

CLASS-II Citizen required an entirely new number and name to match new bodies and lives.

My name and my number are gone. Until I am better I am hardly I. I am a tunnel to somewhere I will be whole again.

The covering still forbids me from moving. I hear more talk of MA and see a tube of blue slip toward me. Mostly, I hear static, whose source I cannot trace. In between, the words "her aggression." Then: "her self-hacking;" "herself hacking." They are lifting an extra arm beside me. That extra arm is mine, or was mine, once. I can see them from my corners, prodding the second stomach that, too, was once mine, then typing on invisible screens. The blue thickens and deepens in color like an ancient gem. Liquid pulses frantically into my body. Blue tubes line my walls.

If I could look at myself today, would I, too, be blue?

They say "her aggression."
They say, "her self-hacking."
My spare arm hangs limp beside my first armpit.
My second stomach is empty, pathetic. Webs of bluest-blue.
Wallwebs.
Frantic entires. So blue my red turned insight out.
Inside-out and sucked away replaced with this.

I was re(a)d before, the color of my scars. They bloomed across my chest and first stomach, my thighs and waist. Skincutting was the first self-hacking I ever did, turning myself a ripe violence, first at home and then in the wilds, emptying my fluids into the river. Generalized self-hacking behaviors had constituted criminal deviance since long before RSCH. Before words became worlds became pens became fences there were already places for the self-hackers to go. The newworld lived already in the old, we learned, in quiet places where proto-RSCH bloomed.

Why had I started the scars on myself? Because the stars blew further before me. Because I was a scar in a longer strike. Because I had no words to know that yet but I knew, I knew I had to have myself. I had to try to have myself and I could only have me if I ruined me, if I made myself a despicable unthing. If I was always defective, I would be the source myself.

EN and DU and 77 could not do this. I do not know what happened to the initials. 77 disappeared behind the shroud of unexistibility, made of itself something they could continue living with. The ongoing trace of the mark I have chosen, they have borne from conception.

The regular bludgeonings came at random. Nobody did them, in order to become somebody again.

(I can't help but wound on the axe. Ruminate the scars. Re-open; massage. Wound. I floss my teeth with it.

have   my own destruction. I could if
given a blade or
a blunt object.)

Of all the things I would have to do. Of all the things I'd be compelled to complete.

The randomness of the axings were the only randomnesses permitted. They were permitted on the condition that they did not occur. That is, the deviant Uncitizens did them to other deviant Uncitizens, so that the former category could re-enter Order. The blood, the axe, all an expulsion of our rough garbage. It could happen in order to peace.

Before the axe we lived in chaos. Chaos tainted every body, rose like thick smokeskin round the best of us, too. We

none of we is I

lived perpetually-proxi-mate to the disorder which would be our ruin. When the axe came down for the first time, when that deviant swung the mythic day toward future, we saw Pure without seeing the dirt. The already-dirty would swing the weapon, axe down contagious kin. Return to health; reject the taint. Uncitizens, soon to be CLASS-IIs, ready to strike into society like the blade of a knife, could do it. Their last gust of deviation before returning to the safe, the orderly.

Without their disorder, we (not I) would lose ourselves. Reya told me many times in the beginning, *they need us*, gripping my arm and calling themself a prefix. Sometimes they would wake in the night screaming, and when conscious turn to me, saying, "it's all on top of me and I can't get out."

Sometimes, Reya felt a phantom bleeding in the empty space their legs once were. According to Reya, they even turned red. At first I believed they were sad about their legs. Reya said they didn't miss them.

"It's not the legs that matter. It's how they went." It wasn't that they were gone, it was the circumstances of their loss. In the mornings after those long leg nights Reya would wake and mutter, *you need me*, before running, crutchwise, as quick and wild as they could.

So RSCH allows the non-axing axing just outside their pur(e)view. Under careful watch no violence occurs but at the edge of doctrine, only to affirm the existence of the laws that keep us safe. As time went on I spent ever-more time in the river, in the trees, hiding behind unwieldy grasses, waiting for the blade to fall on some other body. The sick body falls, another rises, moves a beat closer to transcendence.

> The river, the forest, the blood, they run in the way of the body: contagious. In their slippery murk they promise the path to freedom, transcendence. But transcendence requires discipline. Infection's easy as a dream, simple as a pleasure, which both flowed like oil until forever   dry.

So I was axed to save us all. I was asked to keep the oil in my pocket. I was made infection to fill another's blank. Someone in the Community is a Citizen, now, because I have lost my name. Sometimes I'm too blue to think this way, but I allow myself to ruminate as long as I can stand, for as long as I can pretend I am upright.

I wish I were. Before I always walked through the forest, just for its own sake, just for the sweat of it,

> There was no sweating in the Community, no exertion. It weakened us, RSCH said. Our bodies had to be cherished, like glass or paper, except that now without the glass or paper to cherish, nothing was more cherishable than flesh.

to taste the salt-lick my nostrils became as my legs turned blazing and limp.

For a while I walked but would not eat. Reya insisted I eat what I found laying on the forest floor, the mushrooms they assured me would be safe. I refused. That whole year, if it was a year, I came closer and closer to nothing, blending with the tidy sapling stalks that grew from groundward seeds. Reya held a constant look of terror. I paced often, enjoying how my steps thought the ground, leaving ruminatory evidence in their wake.

Reya begged. Reya's terror grew. We heard the axers and learned to run because we had no choice.

Fewer axers roamed the woods back then. I knew how old I had once been (fourteen years) because I had only just defected; Uncitizens lose their age upon defection. I did not believe I was safe, but I believed I could recover my safety if I chose to, because I believed I had a choice.

That first year I decided I was searching for a history. It was not, precisely, a history I was searching for, because there is only one history and I had already learned it. It was the shape of a thing that held some similarities to real history. I did not know the shape but like the RSCH complex I saw edges whose sideways implications evaded my every thought. (Perhaps when I say I want something like a history I mean I want something like a truth.

I mean a Truth, a cross

I raise in my account.)

I felt unmoored. I no longer had RSCH, no longer looked toward truth through contact lenses. I was below or outside anything real.

Back then I dared some imaginary other to axe me. I craved the pain because I believed the axe was another scar I could use to make myself. Or because I believed if I were small enough, the axe would pass me, I would slip between its blade untouched. I walked outside the paths that generations of deviant feet had carved. I climbed trees and refused to come down, I hung gratuitously, upside-down, from the branches and screamed until hoarse. Reya kept their look of terror. Even greater terror than when they saw the fact of their legs, they told me: watching me walk was like watching something disappear. Meanwhile, I felt something like free—terror felt true. Terror felt like a process I was part of. Even a beginning. If the axe were an end.

My axer lives in a white house now. The axer did not perform the axing that returned them to us, because violence happens outside order. Chaos kills chaos before Order might be invaded. The axer, now a CLASS-II, will not ever raise offspring. Heorshe will not be given an opposite-sex co-guardian. Heorshe will live alone and attend daily meals with friends, as well as the grocery store.

A dr enters. Through the blue tint I see a trainee, whose subordinate status means her face is, for now, visible to all—she has not yet ascended to objectivity. She is as palebright as her blurred superior, a paleness that invents in Pure children

who were not children, but small
arbiters of Truth, whiteness
curled sharp and tight as a fist

the RSCH, dr, police they will be. She has a name   digitally   projected
above her left shoulder, but every time I read it, I forget it instantly. Another
dr enters behind her, addresses her in a name that sounds to me like static.
As they enter conversation, the words turn into data-entry sentences:

My cats are off to the store.

Panda's books are long past due.

Walk inside and bring your basket.

She looks as I'd expect a new RSCH to look. Plush and pristine,
red hair in a braided bun. While I stare into her, she looks past me, perhaps
towards some invisible floating chart. She does not grimace or frown

negative facial expressions are asocial and suggestive of dangerous pathology, so while not entirely illegal, they are severely
discouraged, limited only to situations so unspeakably terrible
as to seem impossible.

But her look is something new. Perhaps fear.

Soon she is caught up amidst a blurry haze of drs, real drs, as they
enter and leave my room in hurried shifts. Time, I assume, passes, at least on
the outside. Here is outside time and outside life. I feel the surface beneath
my back sucking me down into a great, blue cloud.

In the immediate aftermath of the axing, I fell into a dreamstate, sleeping side-by-side with pain and no one else. I thought of Reya, feeling closer to them than I ever had before, as though I were wandering wondering through their field of vision for the very first time; sealing or seeing past-selves walk like ghosts.

I did not see myself. This is the way I became I, nameless, just this frameworking thing. I outgrew the body but remained chained firmly to it. The doctors made white furies around me. Flurries. I saw them as a writhing mass, writing I into a number I would never see. The truth of me became a thing to be hidden, a thing to be concealed until I was ripe. The door opened. The door shut. Texts typed on invisible screens. I called out for my spare arm, my second stomach, but I could not see or feel them. Soon I could not feel my toes or fingers. Then, ankles and wrists. Soon I felt my body only as a vague-pressing weight, an untouchable thing that nonetheless held me still.

They make ghosts through the doorway. When they come close they inform me of my needs. My first need is to say thank-you. My second need is a beverage. The beverage is not the shake (this is my third need) but a liquid blue, so bright I can see myself in it even amid pitch-darkness. Bluer than any sky ever seen. I remember Reya: *don't eat the food.*

I open my mouth to ask why. I receive the blue through a small tube. I went smooth.

When I woke next I was hairless, every final crevice shorn. My upper lip felt raw. My ankles tingled, but I was grateful for the sensation. I did not know what to call this because RSCH did not cause pain. My body did that, my deviant body, growing erroneous hair so painful to remove. Even the space beneath my arms where the nimblest strands tend to grow have been stripped.

There were no clocks in the room. Its walls were windowless. I did not feel like I was inside because I could make no outside. Instead I was suspended, time flattening unless punctuated by drs in white coats.

Later, the darkness began to fade into the color of room-temperature. Still no windows, no visible doors, only the drs entering and exiting as if by will alone. Perhaps they were. Other details remained unknowable, dancing at the edges of my thought. The moment I saw and tried to pin them, they'd skitter away like chalk. I could hardly see where I ended and the walls and floors began.

I felt as if I had forgotten how to speak. All I could do was hear the footsteps, the static, the rare understandable english of the drs reserved for giving me proscriptions. **Attempt speech again and the covering will return.** So I stayed silent. Soon I could not even want to speak. I did not know how to want, only to need, and not to need in myself but to take the need done outside to me.

At first I thought that being here, in the quiet, would give me space to recall all I had forgotten. But each time I remembered, I did not recall. Instead I returned to the place of the memory, torn through it, brought out and duly erased. I did not remember (as I am attempting to do), I was *memoried*. It came in time with the blue. The color came, my thoughts melted. Each time it was a different shade—sky- or lightwater-pale. I felt too-full but at the same time as if something was being emptied from just outside my view. I tried to hold onto Reya. I could not let them slip through to the now-steady sound of beeping machines, nightless dayless days and nights spent windowless in bed. Knowing every movement was tracked and noted.

So I consider Reya. They would be destroyed if they attempted to rescue me. Still, against all logic, I waited for them to come and sweep me away from RSCH like they had swept me from the Community and into the woods. I fantasized seeing them, a specter in the doorway that did not exist. About their presence, spectral in the non-existent doorway. In my fantasy, they were strong enough to disappear   RSCH simply by grabbing it, relegating it to the center of their palm, and closing their fingers. One little unperson bigger than all the impossible lengths of RSCH; bigger than the endless desolate—

No.

Reya sought self-preservation too hotly to come here. So much that—no, no suspicions. **STOP.**

I was so angry at Reya for doing precisely what they ought to do, protect their own survival at my expense. They had been born, failed to comply, the stakes, for them, were far higher than for me. They had squandered their chance, become a waste of resources. **The body is the first crime against the Pure and the deviant live on with impunity**

I knew this. Yet another thought burst forth: *They have all forgotten me.* It wrapped around my psyche until the warmth become suffocation. At this moment the very reddest crevices of my mind assured me I deserved the axing. My body, a crime, the scene , and the evidence. *If they loved you, they would come. But* **you have allowed yourself to go too far** **t h e y want you** *punished*—so shouted the red, curling its dagger into my center, impaling me from the scalp to my toes. *That's RSCH-talk.* I reprimanded it. My face flushed. I began to hold my breath, only allowing myself to breathe when I know I will do so slowly, lowering the rate of my fast-running heart for fear of summoning a dr to my side.

I closed my eyes. While still lucid, I took a memory and placed its contours on the future. Maybe Reya and I would lay together, side by side, and sink into the ground. We would be beneath the trees, absorbing the air everyone else was too afraid to breathe too closely because we were (as always) already polluted.

The walls began to bleed the color blue. A dr appeared at my side. My heart and flush betrayed me. Submerged in blue up to the centers of my eyeballs I heard his voice:

THIS IS THE TIME IN WHICH YOU MUST LEND US YOUR CONTROL WE KNOW WHAT YOU ARE DOING STAY THERE THIS IS THE TIME

They give me a new drink, blue, but navy this time. I am positive the walls are bleeding it. The air is dry, discussing. Blurs around me. Pieces of my underarm skin rip and flake, landing on my dead spare arm. They were afraid to touch me. Averse, I mean. RSCH doesn't fear.

A dr mumbles out-of-code: **do you think this skin will [...] cannot re-do if such a thing is past hope [...]**

> More white coats at the foot of my bed.
> **We must correct this without encouraging— [...] cannot simply encourage others to replace the things they do not like and simply grow**

> I try to ask a question. My voice doesn't work, but they can hear it, or my thoughts. It's difficult to tell the difference.

> *Why are you subjecting me*
> *to this. Do you do this to*

all of the sub   ?

> I could not finish my question. It hung there in the blank space. I had been muted once more. My eyes fell shut of RSCH's accord. Again I tried to tame my heartbeat; showing fear would only encourage them. Is this not what they said of the deviants? **Speaking to their delusions only encourages anti-social behaviors.**
> dr pretended not to reply to my half-asked question, as though the words I semispoke moments before were actually his own thoughts, audified. **It is no good to pretend as though your delusions have merit—it will only make you more difficult to correct.** I pictured him smiling as he said this. I still could not see, presumed that, if I could, he would only be a blur.

> *Do you do this to*

all of the sub   ?

Reya knew something about subjectivity, about being subjected to the worst of the worst. They knew what it meant to be touched and to resist only inside their own head. It's just a relationship, they would always say. It isn't as if RSCH has it all: we're still here. *A speck of power is yours*, I told myself, *even when RSCH has got the rest. They are doing this because you frighten them. Can you believe RSCH can invent you over and over again however they want and you just have to believe it?* At this point I forgot whose words were whose.

I think RSCH will starve if they don't look at me.

I am a part of speech they find fitting into each of their sentences, animating them—

a verb—a vowel?

It feels like being necessary—fear, desire, fear, desire, muddled into one compact ball of heat that floats round the room when they are here with me. When they know I notice, they sedate me until I am cool and clear on the inside.

Reflective without looking back.

8. Life persists.

In the woods, life persists. The forest has trees, flowers, and other dirty wild plants, all of which were illegal to distribute or consume. For this reason, none had names, and as a result, there was no guidebook: what would fill it? Some of the plants could destroy the body, some sickened it, some had a taste I could bear and some did not. We tried our best to leave warnings in symbols and nonsense sounds, to warn the others of the dangerous types, to recommend the pleasant. There were no words for these plants so we used the ones we knew: long, tall, green, brown, short, spiky. The wild held few nouns.

We had stopped consuming plants long before I existed. The Meal Plan Ordinance, designed to keep Citizens "fit, energized, and healthy," forbade us from illegitimate consumption. Consumption of a specially-designed shake thrice daily in the prescribed quantities ensured maintenance of one's target weight, avoiding PBU (Public Burdensome Ugliness) and contributing to the overall health of the Community. Consistent failure to abide by the ordinance through over- or under-consumption would result in immediate treatment. The consumption of wild objects necessitated immediate decontamination processes; oldworld pollutants lingered in the dirt and the water and the deviants beyond the Community's borders.

I was eleven or so when a peer committed size defiance. This was long before my incident at dinner. We were at school. I didn't notice anything wrong with her size, but one day at morning weigh-in, one of the school scales produced a horrible sound and a masked figure—not police or dr or teacher, something I did not know how to name—emerged from somewhere I could not see. She brought a thick white rope around the middle of the girl. The rope tightened. We all gathered around to see her skin leak, just slightly, from the trappings of the cord. The masked woman wordlessly led the girl away, out the door and down the hall, and we could only continue watching until their two forms fully faded.

Our teacher said, "That is what we beseech you to avoid."

That day, at lunch, we received our usual shakes. I stared at mine as if it were a dagger. I could feel it cutting me although I had never, at the time, experienced a cut. Others around me seemed unperturbed, the very lakes of placid light so RSCH-desired. Reya, then-new to our class, was among them.

Our teacher squatted by my side as I stared at the dagger-shake, molten brown in its clear cup. The thing suddenly looked as grotesque to me as the wilds ought to have looked. I knew then the danger of seeing the wrong ugliness.

"And what's going on here?" the teacher asked.

I said, "I'm not sure."

She said, "That's precisely the problem. If you don't follow the Ordinance, you can't think clearly. Of course you won't know what's going on until you comply. Once you do, you will certainly understand this strange error and be glad you corrected it."

My heart quickened. I closed my eyes for a moment too long, begging my body to relent so the rise would not appear on my monitor. But my body unrelenting, as always, did appear, and the teacher told me **it was time to drink or I would get the slice and I would sit here until the both were finished, and if they were not, that I would be sent to RSCH for compliance-training.**

I was grateful to be eleven, still at the age of teachers' grace. To receive warnings and chances. By fourteen it would all dry up.

I drank the dagger and felt my brain burning, burning, burning.

Reya saw all of this happen. Everyone else did, too, but few paid attention unless a warning resulted in a Consequence. Afterward, they showed me their pretend legs.

Reya walked on them like anyone, their long white smock swishing like all others'. No educators noticed, nor did any of our peers. For all the time and space and measurements, for all the moments Reya's secret body faced the eyes of peering authorities, they passed through like a shadow. The smock helped, too, designed to facilitate a compliant appearance.

We stood alone in our secret place and they had lifted their smock above their knees, holding it behind them in one hand.

"Say what you're thinking," Reya said to me, though their eyes did not touch mine.

"How are you like that? You shouldn't—you shouldn't be alive?" I said it like a question and braced for the RSCH reprimand that seemed inevitable. Some small jolt from the contacts, reminding me only full-stops punctuated RSCH directives.

"You shouldn't be alive   " I said, trying to period. Fractal bodies could not exist. "You can't be."

"Right," said Reya, still not looking at me.

"But you're…?" My mind tunneled into itself attempting to recti-fy what I saw. The Uncitizen could not possess a contaminated body. The Citizen's appearance indicated their intrinsic purity. Only Citizens could be alive. Only the living could speak in english. The english of Uncitizens was tainted nonsense.

"I'm not supposed to," said Reya, with an angry smile. Their eyes met my lips. Their smile widened from healthy to delirious. Their teeth were unremarkable.

(We spoke like this, in twiceness. Our place was nonsensical. No one could see, hear, smell, touch, or taste us there.)

"I'm this way because they hurt me," Reya said, smile closing to a forbidden-grimace.

I examined their legs, the precise brown of their thighs. "There must be a treatment."

"A *treatment!*" Reya threw their head backwards, making a prohib-ited sound. Then looked at me seriously, finally, in the eyes. "They did it. I don't care about my legs. But they did it, and I'm not going to say their name, I'm not going to make them real."

The spot evaporated then. I **STOPPED** any intrusion of this con-versation before it entered my thinking, knowing—yet, knowing I could not consciously know—to avoid leaving this out for re-collection.

Reya and I avoided dangerous eye-movements, abnormal gait. This underknowledge was a danger. We performed in a Pure way, making as the makers told a body to be healthy with. Later, we were taught of ter-minally-deviated bodies, whose severed limbs indicated severe psychological defects. Criteria for SLD, or severed-limb disorder, had been expanded to include severance of all bodily protrusions, including breasts, hips, and stom-ach.

Thus breasts, hips, and stomach were limbs with which disidentification, long prohibited, constituted a deviancy unto itself. Frequently co-morbid with other self-mutilatory disorders, severed-limb disorder required permanent patienthood from then on. The Pure body could not be added-to artificially, nor could a body in absence participate in the Community. Each, it was said, went into permanent convalesce. I searched the Imagination for what this may be, but the database, which seemed to contain all real possibilities able to be thought, contained no specifics. For an incorrect Imagination search I was also reprimanded.

Do you remember being into RSCH dream?
Is RSCH dream that has you in or are you
dream of RSCH in its nightmare form? Is a dream
a nightmare always if you have not made it?
The needle the tube the sensitive
be—in the blue I gathered close. My eyes
the blue that makes me

Do you remember the blue, Reya, so heavy
        too heavy to contain, how to carry
this weight upon my back—half of me
is hol   hollo   hollow trunk, I race
to fill

AND WHAT DO I ~~FEEL FEEL~~

~~FEEL~~

, IS THIS THE FEELING?

F

U

L L?

I am thinking about my parents again. My father was unimportant and I have since forgotten him. I remember only his outline at dinner, his footsteps in the hall. I don't remember what my mother looks like, but then, I should not be able to remember that time at all, and only can because, as an Uncitizen, I lost my age.

Citizens eighteen and above leave their guardians' home for their own. Each person's child-hood, the memory storage space where all under-eighteen data is stored, is promptly sorted for efficiency, the unnecessary bits removed—sent, we were told, to a private location. We call it Forgetting, which is different from the act of forgetting

> which, like all other failures of memory, including but
> not limited to false, semifalse, and wrongly-interpreted
> subtypes

is a sign of psychological disorder. Unlike the deviant forgetting, **RSCH Forgetting** was capital, bold as Truth. The removal of the child-hood ensured each Citizen's capacity for autonomy, protecting against phenomena like Parent Codependency Disorder (PCD) a historical epidemic whose sufferers were among the first to defect to the forest. In response to this, and several concurrent events, RSCH established the axe.

drs enter. I try to slate-blank myself. I cannot recall whether or not I have received the blue yet—today? And I don't understand when yesterday or tomorrow will come, whether the two exist from this bed. As a patient, I am outside time, ageless and nonexistent in location. Gloved hands play above my chest, they loosen my gown. I shiver. I want to place this moment in time. But this is not a moment, or, it is not my moment, it is a moment whose passage has nothing to do with me. It is a moment for the drs and for me, nothing at all.

Blue down the pipes. At the site I sweat. This time near-green. Between the waves of it. Now closer to white. I chase my thoughts in circles. I am losing track. I'm losing in the worst way. I used to be leaner, I used to be more supple, I used to memory all to myself. Now I cannot think. My mind, like the arm, like the stomach, like all the parts I grew without the Operator's help. I am a muscle in a trophy   atrophy.

Atrophy. As if you can identify it on feeling alone. You are not authorized to name yourself.

For a flash I see my mother. We are at the store, getting the shake.

Her face remains blank and blurred as a dr's. I feel I am watching someone who is not me, walking at my mother's side.

I have parents. The blue is sickening.

What about them? My parents will not receive a replacement, though RSCH keeps spare sperm and egg cells from each approved couple banked away, stored for the sake of organization rather than use. Each couple gets one chance to produce and rear offspring, for fear of overpopulation and the uncontrollable reproduction of deviance. This was another rule implemented in the wake of familial forest defection.

The order was itself meant to be reproductive. **Citizens ensured the health of the body politic from white house-rows and supermarkets, schools and data centers, all by ensuring individual and interpersonal wellness.**

Two drs, wearing thick gloves whose outlines blur as their covered hands turned to bare wrists, approach slowly. The two blurred blobs of pink and beige in white coats and white gloves lift and measure my spare arm. I hardly feel their lift; the thing must be nearly detached. Another enters with my shake. The trainee follows with a wheeled cart, on which sits a bucket of blue that reaches her waist. She fills the tubes whose edges I cannot see. She extracts a separate vial of fluid from the bucket and places it elsewhere. My shake is set down.

Will you choose to comply?

I cannot reply. I taste an unfamiliar dream, watch my body wander endless foreign halls as white-grey as their ceilings and floors, so vast and long and tangled I feel I am binding to the wall itself. It becomes I cannot tell what is a wall, what is a floor, what is a ceiling. I feel others pass me by, invisible. When the scene turns blue I know it will finish, and I will finish, and I will see another of myself I do not know how to read.

From the walls I hear Reya's voice. I hear the sound of begging, the way they'd hang a plant over my mouth and say *please*, say *stop doing this to me*, as if it were about them at all. Reya's wall-words are impossible to understand. They may belong to someone else. They may be my own. I may be speaking   as I have spoken all this   time

The shake has arrived again. I close my lips, too close to the memory of Reya, the fighting, the shouting, the plants, all my dizzy useless hidings. I do not know if I want them here or if I only want to be what I was—or wished I was—back then. Vanishing.

Thick, sour gloved fingers enter my mouth from either side. As they pull me open I attempt to bite in return, before realizing I cannot bite, I cannot move at all. More fingers enter my mouth and I feel the seams between my lips burning. They pry my teeth apart and place tech between my teeth. The contraption keeps them open while also providing a hole at its center, through which RSCH pours the shake. All the shakes are flavored "chocolate," an oldworld holdover whose precise origins remain unknown.

The shake pits down my throat and to my first stomach, whose existing emptying valve has undoubtedly been disconnected. In my head RSCH rights   writes me let go of control. Let RSCH take control. Let RSCH keep you   from harm. Let RSCH help you protect yourself. RSCH is to help you help yourself. RSCH-based practices help you help yourself. To re-fuse RSCH is to refuse healt   help.   To   refuse health is to refuse help is to refuse health. To Citizen is happy to heal. To be a Citizen is to be happy to be heal   thy. To heal thy self. To Citizen as healthy self. To heal   the body. To heal from the body. To Citizen until heal thy body to out the outside the body.

Is is not the beginning of Process. Accepting what is wrong.

running faster than the light goes.

being underneath.

Letting RSCH take control. Letting rehabilitation manifest. Emerging to the eye. Countable again.

drs speak in garbled english all around me, while the bolded words remain.

Unable to move or speak, hardly able to see but for the swarm of white coats and blurred faces, I know I am re   covering.

axe time runs all ways
　　　　but forward, like slanted,
　　　　　　like compressed,
　　　　　　　　like sideways,
　　　　　　　　　　like out the scream
　　　　　　　　　　　　-open mouth of me
　　　　　　　　　　　　　　as all I see blade
　　　　　　　　　　　　great skin red spots
　　　　　　　　I, but sharp
　　　　　　impact
　　　　a pact
　　　my dark, the price

　　at impact
loose　　　　　　　　me in the moonlit pale
　　make　　　　　steal my mouth
　　make to make to　　　steel

　　　　　night broke cracked through the head dark came down
　　　　　dark matter down knife head down shout down final
　　　　　down sight tween eyes crack crack down ax keep shut

if the body a vestige—if the body a capsule
if the body of made of capsules if the tinder
if the tender closing keeps the ill. if the ill remarks
the husk. if the rip attacks the bit if the bits
uneaten

It wasn't that I liked my body, not even with Reya. It was only that I liked to be felt   by Reya's hands and lips. My body is a dark room and Reya did not feel like a light, not like the eyes and their contacts. Reya felt like a shared darkness, stretching the length of my own. They opened me, pushed my second stomach aside. With them I felt full, but full of something that did not weigh me   down, not even as their body made depressions in my own, little emptinesses whose absence I'd never known to miss.

The first time, I let them lead, figuring they must have done all of this many times before. It seemed that way; they approached all they did with a Truthhood I would only later learn they did not believe. ("I have to make it this way, because I'm no truth. So whatever I do, I have to believe in it.") Our prior thousand not-firsts

They had pressed their hand to the inner curve on my right-hand side, the space which opened to let my second stomach hang free. It was that stomach, that and the first one, that I was terrified for them to touch. An ugly, dirty, gunk-full— the first time I couldn't take it. I had looked at Reya, whose face tried hard not to reveal the length of its hurt. I could not explain myself. I ran up and away. I ran to the tree. I refused their offerings, any of them. They stood naked below me begging. I briefly delighted in their suffering because it distracted from my own.

ghosted round us when it happened.

After that attempt I tried to put my own hand in that space, see if I could stand it. Each time, my fingers found a softness I wished were metal. I should propose to the Operator, "just take the whole mid-bit out and give me a slab instead, no more of this weak, penetrable space full of remnants." Its weakness—my weakness—disgusted me. I traced my inner thighs, my first stomach, the space between; found a wildness my wildself could not take. For Reya to touch the wildness would be to make it real. Not Real, as in RSCH, but real as in the things we placed between us; the things we both chose to see.

In my mind I whittled myself branches for arms and legs and sloughed off all this excess. I did this until I was dead but then remembered you cannot dead a nonthing and so somehow I continued.

"You want to escape," Reya told me. "You don't want to disappear."

"I am escaped."

"We're just between the lines now. Same page."

"Page?"

"We're tied to them."

And axe, bound to happen. Bound into me. I bound to the tree from the river to the mud to the forest and the pieces of the rejects went before me, but I am bound of the axe who stories me. The act I cannot leave.

"You think disappearing will make them stop knowing you. But they have all that memory."

Then I need t   t a   y

But then. The first time. I felt lowercase known. Reya on my hips, thighs, thoughts, center, between. I felt mythic. They   I am
felt   sugar, real sugar   ancient   .
          I felt an archive   of sugar and what I should not
          know.
Their hand dipped down and inward. The space between my legs contained my whole heartbeat. I quivered slightly. Seemingly of its own accord, my spare arm reached out to their other hand, guiding it closer, further, deeper down. This was a sacred moment; a scared moment, reversed. No time passed. It their hands and me and then something more. All was moving and all was still. They went faster, and although I had no idea what they were doing, I knew then that they were better at the body than all RSCH combined, and there was no space inside for boldface, only darkness. In a particularly tense moment, they pulled their hands from me, examining their wet, glowing fingers before placing them inside their mouth.

Again, their eyes closed. Studious. They bent between my legs. There they were, at my very worst angle, watching the hairy softness of my body ripple like an ocean as I shook around them. They moved slightly, balanced on their elbows. I hummed and dulled. After too many dulls, I began to laugh in a way that frightened me; a laugh that felt like the plants I could not eat.

"Your tongue...it's got to be axed," I gasped. Laughter like a whole body in my mouth. They peaked up at me in confusion from below my chest, which was day by day softening, slackening with hormones. Theirs, meanwhile, may as well have borrowed the meat from mine: it grew near daily when the hormones were plentiful and was as sensitive as—

They went back to work, still missing the spot. I continued, "It still has to be axed, Reya. Because…" I was giggling wildly, "It's deviant—it's in the wrong place." I felt laughter, a precious rarity, as their breath hit my inner thighs.

They played along. "Well, then,   " (in the space, they said my name, which I cannot recall), "tell me how to comply."

I moved their head between my two hands and felt their laughter up against my hum. I wanted them to laugh like this forever. Whole body. And then their tongue began to move, and I was, for the moment, relieved at the sudden silence, filling it with little music of my own.

There came a moment, eventually, where all of our selves lined up beside one another. I could see a life I never had, a life they were never offered. I could see us in a house of unspeakable joy. It was not white. It was no color visible. Together we bathed in it, finally opaque, known to no Knowledge but ours. No axe, no eyes, just unarmed hands together.

Afterward I asked Reya if they had felt it, too.

"You couldn't tell by the sound?"

"Not the touch, the thing inside it." The life whose contours I felt I had sensed. The life that had no words to it, not in our english, nothing in the Imagination to explain. The closest thing was comfort, or peace, definitionally opposed to the wild and to us.

"I was worried," Reya said, after a long pause. They continued, but the memory stops here.

The blue looks the way a river feels around the ankle when you know there is only dark beneath but don't know how long it stretches. Tiny surface-changes appear impossibly large from the shore, from the bed. Suddenly I'm no longer on the shore but instead stone, skipping across the surface of it, my body   a machine by others started and stopped. Every tube a throat. Every blue a memory. Every glitch two fingers in a pinch.

"If it was up to me," Reya said, "I would have been born a female,

I think. Just a regular female, without anything else. I could have been born like you and maybe could have stayed. I wouldn't have liked it too much but maybe it would have been okay. I could have at least... dealt."

"You don't really believe you would have liked it, do you?"

"I could have lived, though. I could have been alive."

"And afraid."

"You get the axe if they find you. I have nothing left to mark." Reya rose and reattached their crutches, then pulled on their garment from the pile we had left. They turned their back to me and began to crutch away.

"You can be a woman to me, if you want," I said to their retreating back. "Just like you're Reya." Reya was a *counterfeit*, a name unsuitable because RSCH, whose records listed a cyclically-available list of names (wherein one would be redeployed upon the death of its previous owner), considered it to be so.

"Shut up," said Reya, without turning around. They laughed in two little shouts that made me shiver. They disappeared into the trees.

I knew they would be back. I walked to the river and threw stones at my reflection, piercing each of my parts in turn. My thoughts a brutal chase. I remembered the day I became a woman, the day I was rushed to the clinic, had the offending materials removed and stored. Once, there had been blood, we were told. But we were no longer beholden to contaminatory fluids. Blood was not to be shed.

> When blood occurred during the RSCH procedures it was not shed, but moved, because the drawing of blood was a sign that one was a danger to hisorherself and others. Any sight of it and the police would be summoned, charged with recovering order.

Things like dirt and muck and blood, agents of chaos and pollution, served only to to threaten the Community, bringing inward the hostile outside which the oldworld had destroyed. Reya said RSCH hate the oldworld because they need it, just like they keep us in in order to push us out.

"What I mean," said Reya, "is the same thing I say over and over and no one wants to hear. That they need us. That we aren't just out here wild and alone, that this is all RSCH, too, and that they're right behind—We are DRIVEN, I mean—ensure—"

A cloud of drs all above me. They become drs in my eyes after several blinks, but they have always been drs, because they are RSCH and RSCH is True. I can no longer remember Reya's words to me, everything after ensure secreting from my head. I chase the thoughts, faster and faster, until the inside-sound of RSCH voices take the rest:

What do we do, in such an instance?

I think hard. Reya, wild, RSCH—had Reya said the wild was RSCH? But RSCH was the Facts behind the facts. The Pure-to-the-bottom. The wild was a scourge, as was I. Yet I was made by RSCH, too, even now, unmade by the same.

My first stomach tightened.

Rage responses. What do we do when we witness an affective deviation?

They ask and do not ask me. The cover goes over me again.

FAILURE TO COMPLY

The world outside was dead already, and of its death RSCH made the truth. On the outside was all gone   past hope; even all those spectral dead things existed only by RSCH's tongue. If RSCH did not name the outside, the outside was not, and thus we should be grateful, because we have a history.

The wild has its own sort of history, an anti-history mostly made of mods. The mods to our bodies modded the history itself, so that the story we walked refused RSCH-fit. And we made it holding each other, Reya on my spare arm as we foraged, breaking briefly to fill our haphazard baskets with plants before connecting again. Other Uncitizens sometimes passed us

Few walked together, none congregated in large groups, an act forbidden to Citizens and dangerous for deviants, whose inherent dangerousness increased exponentially when in another's company.

When the few who did pass saw us, they saw a response to History. Our modding of it. Our walks did that, respond, make a winding text of the trail. Like I do now, chasing my thoughts as they leave, unsure whether I am driving them out or attempting to keep them in, and if in, where, and for what?**NO**

We would walk until we reached the rejected bodies. They lay near to RSCH's impossible wall, in a small clearing lined by skinny trees. **Tainted from the sickenened bodies.** The soil smelled like metal. The soil rippled with the hacked bodies at the very surface, some hardly covered by dirt. Who knows how deep the buried went. Above, the RSCH wall seemed to creep outward, step by step, each time several fewer moments from consuming us.

Below our feet lay defectives new and old and neither because there was no time; the wall marked the edges of time and we were out. Defectors like us, broken into soil rendered toxic under RSCH eye, or RSCH wall, which could just as well have been made of infinite invisible perpetual eyes whose sights could seize at any moment.

Reya would busy themself before the wall, pretending not to be afraid. I don't know if they feared RSCH itself more, or the RSCH in the chip on their neck. They would pick and pick around the chip until they drew enough blood to thicken their fingernails.

"Why are they all *here*, though? So close to everything?" They gestured at RSCH with a bloody hand, crutch waving below. "Why the Purest space, right here in the wild?"

I had also been shocked at first. Rejects lay a few strides from an impossibly-sized site of truth. Rejects right between the lines, right in the shadows, darknesses RSCH could not, in fact, emit. Because of their impossible size, RSCH facilities could cast no true shadow. The bodies below were simply shrouded in dark.

"When I end up here," Reya said, "and you know I'll end up here, put me far enough down so that people won't try to dig me up and look at me."

They began picking at their chip, but harder this time, making little shovels of their fingers.

In a flash came burst blue spilling drowning the scene from blue an axe manifest as if by   as if by as if by dream

promotion of anticompliance
even by one individual, inhibits
collective recovery.

9. What would become / RSCH.

The first deviants came about   / always have been. They became apparent in the specificity of their deviance at the early formation of
what would become /

comprise / call itself / be / turn to   RSCH. Armed
with evidence-based techniques to skillfully discern objective truths, RSCH
noted the indisputable correlation between environmental and social contamination. The deviance already located in some bodies, they found, was
being exacerbated by what those bodies consumed. Water, polluted. Sun, hot
and reddening. Food, grown in backyard rhizomes, without order or align-
ment. A long series of unspeakable events led to the rise of mass deviation,
the collapse of the social order. We need now only know RSCH was savior.

Still, I wondered what happened to them. The first ones, who refused
the shakes early on. Soon, when they treated the gardens, the gardens would
not grow, but this was the fault of the plants themselves. They preformed
a strike, using Food-Restricting Behaviors (FRD) and refusing the shakes.
Mothers drank illegal water and had their strange babies out of their bodies,
secreted them to the woods. Secreted all their juices as they ran, leaving trails.
Even still, it seemed they were difficult to kill, never any more than the shadow of a real—that is, living—that is, killable thing. Deviance was difficult to
kill because it was already dead. Many died all the same.

I imagined where they went, where they may have gone, or if they
all lay underground for good. Underground, perhaps, was something other
than RSCH eyes—ever-on streetlights running on concentrated solar power,
ensuring that eyescanners work no matter the time of day, letting no one go
unnoticed or uncounted.

The deviants are the shadow, but the shadow is still a thing, even if the thing
of the shadow is no-thing. The shadow is different from the Outside, which
is a nothing that simply isn't. RSCH spans the whole of the real, which is the

size and shape of a large dome. All has been mapped; even the unmapped
wild   designated as such and thus mapped and its own   shadow way.

Those not brought beneath the dome back when the oldworld entered History and the rest entered the future simply ceased. RSCH, recordkeeper, declared them gone.

But where did they go?
Where did they go if they
did not comply, before history started and before the
Community was the Community, before RSCH was
everything? To imagine outside a shattering darkness.

I hear footsteps from my bed. I bury the thoughts like bodies. I know
my rising heart rate is evidence enough, but still I attempt re-covering. I hear
indiscernible shouts, feel something strange against my chest, then feel that
something—a hand, it seems—cringe back from its flatrock surface.

I think good thoughts. I think I think good thoughts and so they
are brought to pre-existing awareness as to my conscious thinking of good
thoughts, which is healthy in its recognition of RSCH doctrine but bad inasmuch as it is unnatural, that is, artificial, that is, an artifact of a time before
we knew the Truth for what it was.

More footsteps. I was having trouble summoning words. There was
no access to the Imagination here, not for Uncitizens. It was impossible to
search without the database. Like remembering words in the other longdead englishes that once existed outside, their words now defunct in the face
of the truth-making set. Long ago they had been run through translators,
now-defunct pieces of tech that turned deviant englishes into intelligible
ones. Translation is what made RSCH. RSCH continues its translation, this
time turning bodies into texts and into archi   text

A blurred dr withdraws a tube of midnight-blue. Heorshe tips my
bed backward until my legs are above my head. They know how to feed, how
to force, how to punish. More blue enters me. My mind is awash with it. I
can hardly h   I can hardly hold my faculties. I look for a thing

to remember. Each I pull fades immediately. I try to remember every body I have been. I remember the surgeries that brought me here and made me wild, each a spectral comfort and a terror. These, some lingering terrors even to myself, flush from me.

We lay you this way to achieve balance, to cure the depression in your heart. STOP racing your thoughts. RSCH, the archive, will win.

RSCH took hold by preying out the sadness. If the world was a body we were being stripped naked by the sun. Solar production went into overdrive. Populations grew risky—that is, in need of management. **Until we figure out what's going on**—the population is getting more and more disturbed, bodies growing into unrecognizable shapes—we have put a moratorium on reproduction; no knew   new people until we know how to deal with them. Temporary, of course. I don't know what tense to talk this in, but this is how it begins.

Then, the mass-wellness interventions on the already-living. Just as history began, we were still primitive; masked axers ran into classrooms and offices, using reason and, inevitably, (because the deviant is unreasonable) force to remove contagion from environment. A schoolgirl crying at a bad test grade. A child, playing with hisorher food, refusing the shake. A teenager, voice loud against their parents, perhaps even speaking a foreign english. Parents, unwilling not to procreate. All into a van to body into data; to be worked and molded by the rest to sentences. They were treated in life-sentences.

This was not so long ago, but as soon as RSCH happened it was pre-history and myth, compulsory as a means of telling Truth   from lie. RSCH had implemented the PD (psychologically disciplinary) curriculum in all schools to prevent such occurrences as the roundup from ever happening again. Or perhaps the occurrences they referred to were the deviants ourselves. Themselves. Who RSCH made   made off with made up.

The lesson was this: in the event of an epidemic like the one that birthed the Community as we know it now, an equal and opposite suppressant force must be employed. This was before the contact tech was discovered, so RSCH made memory in other ways: the cameras on our front doors and electronics. The heretofore unknown option built into the then-new HoloScreens, which allowed simultaneous projection and observation.

Early intervention began with the parents, some of whom had never guarded any child before but were fortunate enough to have passed RSCH's new fitness screening, meant to select orderly people, to (re)make order from chaos. Their emotional minds were kept in check by the rational, their faith placed accurately in RSCH's capacity for progress. They possessed the disciplined minds through which ultimate transcendence of the body may one day be achieved and the sickly porous kin will finally be shed. RSCH used evidence-based methods to ensure their continued fitness. They considered the relative wellness Though the mind will require discipline until the body is transcended—the body being the site of contamination by the wild, the dirty, the defective—it can be optimized through specific, evidence-based measures. Each well-parent was a piece of evidence. Collectively, they were called a body. This is the only desirable type of body: the completion of neatclean truths without any leakage.

The leaky bodies were dismissed, those who could be mended stayed. The sun turned nearer and time was quick. The Community was made, that is, RSCH was made, because RSCH is the Community, every bone of it. Well-people translated into Citizens. The deviant to patients, unrecovered and contagious. And the space between was called the evidence-base.

what is unseen —
scene, the shadow text
casts, detritus sloughed of
f histories

what must prowl
below real
because to o real
is wrong of prowl

        is to walk
        is to foreward
        ahead
        mere happenstance body

In a dream, I found myself standing up. There was a table with my meal replacement in front of me. There were five other seats at the table, all occupied. Now I was the sixth. I sat. The other bodies at the table were not mine, but to me looked like they could be: they looked the way I imagined myself to look, not in the mirror but from RSCH, from nowhere and everywhere. They looked like what I thought the truth of me to be, which was, of course, inherently-untrue, because I was thinking it.

Some of me were sipping dutifully; I leaned in and examined the way other-me's eyes blankened and lolled with each sip. Another me left the bottle unopened, staring pointedly at nowhere (or everywhere, or RSCH). Another spooned the drink directly into her second-stomach. All of them still had the stomach, though only that one seemed to notice its existence. A knife manifested in my—my dreamself's—hand and I punctured the bottle in front of me.

Another me drew a utensil from nowhere and held it to my neck, as if I were now the bottle. I wanted to tell her I was the opposite of the bottle: I was loose, small, and even nothing. I was full of nothing because I was nothing to fill. I raised my jaw, daring her to do it. She was bluffing. I knew. I had difficulty hurting other bodies, even if they resembled my own.

A different me reached to pat my arm, but before her fingers could reach me, some black thing separated us, fast as a shadow. It expanded. At first it looked like a flattened, two-dimensional portal, but widened into a hole in its own right. Imagine a great black space o

n the page instead of a sliver to crawl through. Imagine a crawlspace with no end and the whole is so dark it may not be there at all, it may merely be the projection of an absence too absent to exist. We, she and I, mirrored each other from either side of the black chasm.

She looked at me very precisely. I struggled, but met her uncontacted eyes. She lifted her meal replacement, raising the fingers of one of her hands, closing them gradually as seconds passed. Five, four, three, two, one. She held it to her lips. A bluff. She thought she had me convinced she was going to down the drink if only I did as well. *What was this*, I thought to myself. Animating a deviant to convince a deviant to drink. Where in my data had they found the parts to make this dream, and why, in the midst, was I capable of realizing it?

One of the six of me drank the shake in full. I realized all were watching my exchange across the chasm. The one who drank shifted on her feet before falling in. The blankness swelled and exploded. The scene wept blue from its edges, tinting our skin.

There was no winning this test. If I refused the shake, I would be noncompliant. If I relented, I would have relented to the advice of a deviant, rendering whatever it was I did, however rational, irrational at its very root, contaminated by its origins.

I wake with no memory of the events immediately preceding this dream.

We lay together and did nameless things, even when the axe seemed just around the next tree trunk, behind this or that thick of leaves. Without legs to hold my head they simply shook and bashed me with their thighs. I found nothing for it in the Imagination, no word, no song for the smell and taste and strange sound of their voice. When it was me on my back I couldn't think about anything, never mind an english for my feelings. I wondered if, like our private schoolspace, our un-Imaginable doings here placed us just far enough beneath the truth to go, for a time, without notice.

They would pull me up in between our shaking, press their lips to my face and neck and everywhere, sucking my sweat away. They gasped the salt-taste into my mouth. We swallowed and swallowed and swallowed until it seemed we were permanently enlodged. Something past between our bodies through the brown earth which turned beneath us, the green and yellow strands of OldGrass. Something grew.

"Remember when the boy asked about people with neither?" Reya stared down their body at themself, suddenly pushing my hand from its resting place across their ribs. At the time we had both grown lean for lack of hormones and a scarcity of vegetation.

"He, the boy, was talking about me. He saw something. He did the thing we're all supposed to do. He saw and said something. Except, he did it on himself. When he looked at me he saw the—the not even deviant, the never-person, he couldn't see his reflection."

He had tried and tried to conjure Reya's name and, at a loss for english, said only his own.

"What do you call it?"

"*It.* That's what I was—all they meant to talk about was my it. But my it was all there was, so I became it."

"And now?"

"Now I'm Reya. Which is a lot like *it.* Because the sounds don't mean anything, they're just sounds, no english for them. They don't exist unless RSCH decides they do. Everyone's *it,* there, even if they come back. They're the problem and the problem is it and it needs to be fixed. Once it's fixed, maybe heorshe again."

"You've put a lot of thought into this."

"It's all I've ever thought about."

They went quiet, then went shaking, but this time in a different way. I held them as they made more sounds, this time terrible. I kept their body still   until they could return.

"And the monitors, I'm sure he had them. Did I tell you about the monitors? There's a division in there that just supervises special cases, kids, that don't go away for RSCH but cannot be trusted alone. Well, not kids, because we're its. It's called PAM—Purity Adherence Monitoring. It used to be a girl's name before the regulations. The guardians have to submit you to PAM, and then PAM is your only official 'guardian' for a while. The result is the same, though. Correction or disposal. PAM is just...well, it's the same old thing, just pronounceable this time."

"Just say RSCH, Reya."

"No one 'says' RSCH. You didn't even say it. Wrong letters."

RSCH was an ever-open mouth.

"I didn't get much PAM, because my MA—misplaced aggression, everyone was going in for that—was severe, low-functioning. Went in quickly. I still remember the voices, the blurring."

I was stuck on MA. There had been a variety of associated symptoms, not required for a diagnosis but helpful as supporting evidence. In the past they had tried to diagnose MA in those who touched the walls of their houses; extended contact between hands and walls correlated with high aggression. This was duly dismissed in time, as more observational equipment was put in place. When sensors sat in every wall in every home, hand-to-wall contact decreased on its own.

"... And they spoke of me, or of 'it' that I remember, and they said—I can hear it, they said—"

Reya seized, almost toppled from their already-seated position. I reached to steady them, feeling tiny lumps emerge beneath each hair on their thick-covered arm. They righted themself, then, holding my shoulder with one hand.

"You don't need to tell me what they said," I told them. And then I waited for them to tell me. They said nothing.

"I can't wait for the day I can shrink RSCH so small I can hold it between my thumb and pointer and tell them their names for me are no better or worse than my own," I continued, imagining them, their mouth, the mouth of Order, in my place. I pinched my thumb and index finger in front of my eye, crushing a large brown shrub.

Reya stared far away, likely trying to resist a chip-resurgence. Successive episodes only made the subsequent ones worse, we knew. Their look reminded me of the way contacted people looked at me, the way I had been expected to look at them. Meet their eyes, then look past, see their stats. Reya looked into the treelined sky like making stats out of a body, like making a memory they can bite, perhaps hold.

The events preceding the implementation of the shake-only nutrition regime were unqualified natural disasters. Poison entered our water sources, toxins rapidly infected major food sources. Deviant "communities," made by fugitive self-hackers, escaped patients, and other enemies of RSCH, sprung up in the darkest and least contactable places. RSCH sought them out in an attempt to provide re-integration and Citizenship recovery services. The places where the deviants stayed turned uninhabitable

> (but they always were, homes of deviants   of   deviance, but the fugitives fled and plants in seconds rotted in the ground and water turned grey and brown and black and yet somehow they were already   infected

RSCH began mandating the consumption of nutrition shakes in order to avoid the deadly effects of poisoned crops. They developed a shake to provide "complete nourishment" to the general population: all healthy Citizens' bodies would respond positively in terms of shape and size to the shake. Those whose bodies did not betrayed their deviance naturally. A certain segment of the population could not tolerate several of the shake's ingredients. They were nullified quickly and quietly.

Before it was fully implemented, a group of activists

> the early term denoting those who resisted RSCH orders of rest-as-wellness, instead committing individual, strenuous acts of bodily abuse which further damaged the collective.

grew   rowdy.

They began showing up at RSCH centers and accosting RSCH themselves, who walked among the Community with visible faces, not yet in possession of Objectivity. The activists demanded to be called Citizens.

At this time in the school lesson, we would be permitted to laugh.

Early deviants, we learned, did not want to be exiles. They became exiles because RSCH declared them to be so and because RSCH was correct; they were false and had no business mingling with Truth.

The deviants now take up exile with a sense of pride, perhaps belonging. Reya felt themself amid a long line of something, part of a many they brought with their body. We knew them only in legends and dreams, in myths and untruths prior and outside of history.

What did they do before the start of history? What do we do when we build outside it? Activists took to RSCH claiming they—and here again, the students may laugh—*they* were the true foundation of the Community. They brought their filthy pieces, crutches and pretend limbs and energy-boxes and strange pills and fluids to the doorsteps of RSCH and called it kindling, a word in pretend-english (english prior to being tended by RSCH authorities) whose origins remain unimportant.

They sprayed their fluids in the faces of RSCH.

They screamed and made shapes with their bodies.

They even—and here we hear a whisper in the history, so low we will not be tainted in the very process of hearing—obliterated themselves before the very drs because of whom they lived. Someplace in their backwood wilds they had lost their minds.

Mind-loss, RSCH later concluded, was terminal.

I could see it happening at the edge of my sight. My site all blue my site all blue-grey like the inside of my open mouth. The color of the darkest sky I'd ever see, a blue too dark to see beneath but just light enough to squint and see your outline, just light enough to call you into being.

After a lifetime on the shake, the wild food hurt my stomach. I believed that its poison would poison even me, the toxin itself. My body rejected the plants even when my mind, at last, relented, but when my body did rejection I felt as if my mind was being sliced open the way my digestive system was. The second stomach helped: a storage space, where plants could degrade and return to my flesh, the next time with fewer scars.

The water was worse in all the anticipated ways. Only with time did it relent.

All of it was unsafe. I spent what RSCH may count as days or weeks laying on the forest floor, pinned in pain. Yet like the surgeries (many moved directly from the Operator's sighted hands to the rejected forest) it was an unsafety we took on. It was an unsafety that already afflicted us. We were past everything. Past known. Unknown is unseen is unsafe, and so the pain we felt was a price of our relentless unknownness. Ghosts injecting ingesting ghosts   pain eating   pain. It felt not

better, but more survivable   (because   the
already-dead survive forever)

      nothing cannot kill nothing
      nothing cannot starve
      nothing cannot expell   nothing has truth

      fully gone

I suppose I'm resisting something. Resistance impedes the flow of progress, and I do so by remembering and by disremembering. I am packing all of what I might want to remember away somewhere I can dig up in case the   what I fear. Earlier, I resisted gloved hands on my body with my two functional, shaking fists, until they were put down and I forgot what the gloves were doing, why I was so angry, and could only chastise my own MA behaviors before falling unconscious.

I think about resistance as a wall, a wall that can endure much force acting upon it without moving (or, perhaps, the force itself is the resistance and the wall is whatever it must push against). This is a wall I choose to touch. It's a wall I occasionally forget, now more so than usual. I am trying my best to record   re cord   so later I will tie it to whatever I is then.

I think they are trying to take my eyes, because my eyes allow me to see the wall that stands between me and the outside. I could not always see the wall, but lately—if, outside time, there is a lately— it has manifested and now I cannot unsee it. I did not realize that other subjects couldn't see the wall until I saw the bewilderment on drs' faces when I asked what on or off of earth the wall was made of. And then my mutation, as usual.

They also do not know I can see something slipping from the top corners of the walls down to the floor, creeping ever-closer to me; leaving in its wake a breathless nothing. I think it underneath my thoughts, which is where I store the public record, which I record to you and I.

Some walls are symbols of far scarier things.

> There is a wall between Purespace and wildspace, though it cannot be seen or heard or felt. The wall is poisonous. It stops most defectives before they even manifest their defective behaviors, before their defectivity becomes apparent in their defection to the forest.

From the tunnel I dig I remember before this room, for the first time, and I burrow deeper into this cavernous space which seems to be out of my mind. I remember the intake exam, a scene between the axe and the blue. Am I the I who lived the scene? Am I, now? I know

I was still allowed to walk on my own back then. I walked into a mid-sized room, empty of all furniture but a large cubby containing a shining silver desk and matching chair. I sat right in the center of it, posture perfect out of reflex. Though this arrangement was new, the test's medium was de-cidedly old-fashioned: I was provided a simple ink pen and piece of paper, double-sided. I marveled at the paper, a rarity illegal to produce without RSCH approval. We learned pen writing with inkless styluses on electronic notebooks, but this, I soon realized, was hardly similar to the pen I then used.

I picked the pen up, held it, placed it at the leftmost point of the topmost line, a blank space directly following the first of the intake battery. I set out to carve my first letter when a shock streaked through my hand. I dropped the pen, trying not to cry out. In the silence of the room I heard: **You will not proceed until you hold and exercise your pen cor-rectly.**

I tried five times. The sixth I did not get a shock. Finally, I could read the question preceding the blank:

Y/N: DoYouHaveTheDesireToAdjustYourPhysicalForm?

It came to my mind all at once, the RSCH question and the impos-sible I was beneath it. If I circled Y, they would write: "subject retains desire to impurify self via self-modding." If I circled N, they would write: "subject is resistant to purification and treatment efforts." Long deliberation times were suspicious, too. "Subject appears calculated in attempt to ascertain the correct answer, instead of the truthful answer." The longer I considered this, the more suspicious I became. I started to shake, and though I did not touch its edges, the flanks of my cubby shook too.

Footsteps passed behind me, first crescendoing and eventually fad-ing, only to return in what felt like moments. My back tingled. I could not turn around for fear of engaging in paranoid behaviors, nor could I pause until the footsteps were gone. After all, they would not go, they would simply pause an unknown distance from my body.

Y/N: I believe this body requires improvements.

A hot gaze on my shoulder blades. If I say yes they will say that is **indicative of my self-modding behaviors tendency** and if I say no they will say this indicates that I have no hope of recovering

my body, the Pure one that I so

nearly disposed of.

when improvement is improvement because it is maintenance of
what should be

re-covering all its pre   seeding absences

Still shaking, I attempted to select. Then, a booming voice, this time
undoubtedly

**It has been thirty minutes. Your Citizenship and re-inte-
gration intake questionnaire will conclude in**

I felt a black spiral curling down, inside my head, deep into my
throat. It was as though I was speaking their directives to myself. How did I
get here? Am I in here at all? Am I happening **You have fifteen minute-
syou have** fifteen   How did I get here and where did I come
from? Where was I before the cubby? Have I ever seen the outside of it,
have I ever been without the guard whose footsteps gather at the base of my
moment?

You have ten minutes. This time it was my own voice, inside my own
head. Was this a trick? I cannot trust the voice inside my head because it is
defective, and yet it says what RSCH does, and yet it cannot, because when
RSCH says it simply tells the existing and immutable Truth**Five minutes
remaining**

I think myself into a hole. Finish the exam, answer every question.
The footsteps. The shooting pain of eyes in my back, eyes around, eyes above
and below and my own eyes, inside me, doing the work of the rest. I rise, just
for a moment, upon answering the final question.

**Do you understand the nature of your prior failure to
comply**

I am surprised I can stand. I look above the cubby and into a shattering lightness. I attempt the Imagination, already locked, so I
can make the image of my monitors, as if I am the camera.

and commit to re-attaining a healthy lifestyle?

As if I am the eye I imagine.
And I see

small speakers
; mount
ed on the wall; so black they were
difficult to see amidst the dim.
Shockingly small. Again came the sound
of walking feet. The old-fashioned speaker, perched
and yelling footstep-sounds, was certain
ly in need of a tune-up.

itself
a   discard

The text returns to me   now
suddenly disordered,
and I suffocate
          sink
until I am
the bed the cold the
 cold   tileme beneath
tile
      deep into
 bed
stand again   will never
            tileme the
        sinking me so deep
 pressing to the every
thing is
 from all sides of my eyes
and hardly feel the needles
I hands,   hardly hear
the questions   I nod
    hope   speak
voices   fear   I am
speaking with their voices
    mine gone
    why   why is my voice
a bed
    underthing

EXCERPT
THE PURITY COMMISSION
[CONVERSATION BETWEEN DR. 3238 & DR. 10390]

10390: We have retained all documentation on the subject in question specific to our laboratory, as well as several years of EyeScan data and location-tracking. Subject left the Community grid several years ago. I have called you in not to rehash previous conversations on Subject, but instead to raise you a new concern.

3238: I worry they are multiplying.

10390: As you know, I've two primary tasks: to remain here for the next twenty-four hours, and to send out a disciplinary note, the latter of which I have already done. Are you sure you can be trusted to do such important work if you yourself remain enslaved to your worries? Your worries that will not productively counter the rising tide of deviance which threatens our borders?

3238: I am—is this—

10390: Are you attempting to euphemize your fear? Is that fear? Is that fear of the specter of the outside that we discover truth in order to guard against? There is no fear in Truth. Truth is without feeling.

3238: No, not fear. I feel concern. I know we have become more than our history. We will never be less again. I believe in the glory of our collective will as it has turned last civilization's nothingness into our present state of prosperity and, most of all, Knowledge. I only note the widespread degeneration, the startling uptick in psychopathology.

10390: It has turned profanity into Citizenship.

3238: Of course. But—

10390: And to remain the topmost of all civilizations on all potential universes, what do we do?

3238: Rise from animal to Citizen. Know the alien before it knows itself. I only think perhaps—

10390: I may record in my notes for this meeting that prolonged, unmediated contact with the deviant may weaken the will of even the Purest Citizen, dr.

Have you fallen prey?

Have you been listening?

It's cool here. The woods are in my eyes but the sensations in my body belong to RSCH. This is a comfort. If I had the energy I would distrust, but to distrust in RSCH is a deviance I cannot do. I feel limp, wrung out   of text.

Vision clearing, I now see a memory   a girl   in a stall beneath a platinum nozzle. There is water falling from the ceiling. There is water from the floor. She is being bisec te   d sexed by the water. Goes through her half by half. Hands enter the stall. Touchmove. She has no head but I can tell she'd scream if she could. In the space where there is her head there is more water. She'd have to scream if it were a mouth. But now she was living inside a scream, the stall a vertical mouth. She has a head but may as well not, because there must be nothing in there. I don't know her but I know that scream. I want to believe it's Reya. It isn't. Reya bathes themself in the mud because the water hurts them in ways I don't understand. I know the scream. I know the sound. This is too hard to be a memory so it must be a new vision.

Here is the hallway. I hear low chatter around me. I try to vocalize *I'm here* but know wherever I am is not here, it's there; alien to the intimate.

I try to introduce myself but forget my name.

I hear a distinct voice amid the chatter and wonder allowed   how long it had been here.

Long enough, it says. It also has no name.

It continues in this way until the outside feels more a dream than inside, the lines of blue and tubes and wires a senseful forest of themselves, my limbs limp weighted branches and my body a body   sinking beneath reason's soil.

A voice wakes me from remembering. **You are not to speak. We have removed your isolation band as a compliance-reward. If you prove yourself unable to be trusted, then it will return indefinitely.**

awake i hear the word "triage"
reminder   i feel good
as dead.
reminder   smell of the rust
of the axe of the
survival of triage is a
reminder   a hearty dent
an in - to my heart

10. The Operator sewed a mouth.

The Operator sewed a mouth. I don't know whose, but I know she was chalky and hollow in all the ways I wished to be, back in the beginning. What raw, innocent pain I felt, living amid a clueless abjection I did not know how to think. It was RSCH in my head, RSCH law mapped to my body, but flipped inside-out and poked with skewers and chopped in pieces and fed until I blew. I had no words for any of it, yet I gave myself to its familiarity.

Still, I'd never have my mouth sewn. I speak too much, and I only know a few of the symbols some make with their hands; artifacts (artificial, that is, untrue, facts) of an oldworld english.

I could see the benefit to a sewn mouth. With RSCH hiring, we were all on high alert. There must be more defectors, more people getting found and chopped. There was talk among the Uncitizenry of speculative

That is, concerning untruth.

drones to better survey the wild. This, even though drone usage was restricted to the borders of the Community (which drones themselves discovered-drew) so as to avoid contamination. I did not know if the drones would come, but I watched mod requests grow more desperate. A sewn mouth and stopped scream might help her hide from the axe, especially given RSCH knowledge of our voiceprints, only modifiable via ever-rarer hormone supplements.

The Operator began with her tongue. She gave its cut her permission by pulling with all her might on the tongue and gesturing wildly toward it while the Operator watched with its eyes-for-hands extended straight out, pupils spinning wildly within twin glass cases embedded in its palms. Then she screamed and the trees shook with it. She screamed until she didn't.

When the tongue departed, it did not remain in the Operator's bloody eye-hand but dropped to the ground, wriggling like a living thing. Hopping through the dirt. Entering the filthy river. Turning all the water part-saliva.

I followed the tongue, having had enough of the operation. It danced through the river and I did too, first walking then skipping then loping, that is, running like an animal, as if the tongue and the river were animals and I was an attempt to join. When the tongue landed once more I reached out to grab it. It almost slipped away, but I held firm and still. It wriggled the way my body would if my body could wriggle without me, pleading for its own eradication. It begged (of) itself: *please remove that thing.*

I was generous with the voice I gave it, lacing its plea with the notion of all the expletives I didn't know, the filthy oldworld words long since condemned out of history. Little emptinesses like running tongues. I dropped the thing into the water. It splashed as if they were english. For each splash a word unworded.

Tongue gone, I returned to Reya through the darkening forest, hands outstretched as I made my way. When the way grew too fast for me to make I began to run as if unmade oblivion tailed me, as if the water that swallowed the tongue would get me, get mind, get   mine, too.

I ran until Reya stopped me. It was dark enough that I could only see Reya's outline and the whites of their eyes. The only light came from the nearly-invisible street lamps lining the borders of the Community.

We lay side by side then, in our invisible patch. Reya unlaced their crutches, placing them beside their body. Then, I felt and heard them rummaging. They leaned toward my ear.

"Drop it."

"What?" I asked.

"Put it on the ground."

My spare arm obeyed them, even as the rest of me remained confused. In the hardly-light I saw my third arm drop a slice of wriggling pink into the grass beside me. Reya leaned over me, dropped a tiny white pill right on the center of it, which set the whole thing steaming. The noxious steam beat my face until, finally, the night was silent again, and I knew the tongue—the somehow-tongue, hear   of someone else's accord, had made oblivion forever. Perhaps for good.

I hardly slept that night, kept awake by their fitful moaning and half-mumbled dreams, and forgot to ask about the steaming capsule. But when Reya finally awoke from a brief moment of sleep, they looked me in the I until eye ached.

"I keep them in case."

"In case what?"

They gave me a look so brutal I wanted to swallow the words. There were things about Reya I never wanted to know. Yet these same things pushed me further toward them. I couldn't help but ask.

Reya turned away from me, gathering a pile of roots they had foraged the day before and raising the topmost to their lips.

"Did you hear about the woman who got her mouth sewn up?" I asked.

They passed me a root and said, "It's not going to happen."

I gnawed without biting.

"Yes, I heard the screams until it closed her up for good, and after that the other noises. It's not going to help, she's still going to make sounds, just muffled ones. Anyway, we have to move. Especially away from that," Reya nodded at the nearby remnants of the tongue-puddle. Or, rather, the nonremnants: where the tongue once was absence remained. Not empty space   absence.

"We're going to have to go deeper," said Reya. I didn't know what "deeper" meant—further from the borders, whose boundaries did not manifest materially but were spoken into Truth? Further, then, toward the ends of everything, to the glassy edges, against which the absent outside pushed against the toxic wild?

"We're going to have to go now, too," Reya continued. "Do you hear it?"

I heard. Deeper, then, meant further from the axe, whose sound echoed from somewhere nearby. We picked up our remaining roots and walked inward, that is, outward, that is, toward the polluted so polluted it obliterates. The borders outside of which I dream and when I dream I see a wall. The wall is a room without windows and I am blue within it.

I'm naked.

I cannot undress the wall.

From my bed I'm moved to test strange instruments, grabbed my second stomach, third arm and first rest and measured, gloved, lingered, refused, w   axed, moved to a transparent table whose existence I only know sturdy beneath me. Like a border I have never seen it but I know it is there because I am not on the floor.

When I am finished lying on the clear surface I get the question.

Do you desire to alter your physical form?

I consider my response, but unthink my consideration of it.

I wish to alter only in accordance with RSCH protocol.

RSCH alters no body. RSCH restores the Citizen to hisor-her natural state. RSCH prepares for transcendence.

The same catch-22, the same dilemma, the same exam I could not pass. It becomes difficult to remember the place I was before this room. It is hard to believe I am still there, out there, that some part of me is scattered still.

I woke up to realize I had forgotten Reya's face and my own.

From above, I am watching someone work. I cannot tell if this is my dream or RSCH, or if the distinction matters anymore. The woman I watch is an adult. Whoever she is, she looks like something beautiful and ought: beige, correctly-shaped, with a normative weight-to-height ratio. She does not look like me, but looks the way I could be if I were Purer. I still cannot remember my face but simply know she is a better vision of it (this could be RSCH).

RSCH takes her out of storage.
Piece by spotless piece.
Shining every joint, plucking every hair, and here she is, appearing to have been born that way. My image
shuts.
I am looking down from above at only her. The image surely isn't mine.

She wears only loose white garments that bunch at her wrists, ankles, and neck. She sits surrounded by screens, entering numbers by touchpad. The touchpads are flat, glowing and cyan-backlit. The screens are glowing white. The ceiling is uncomfortably close to her hair, which has been pulled from her face and covered in a loose, netted cap. This is the standard data-sorting costume, donned by each adult Citizen everyday at work once past security; street clothes folded for later and replaced.

A passage appears onscreen, and then another, and then a video. Data, copied down, organized, and promptly forgotten. The videos speak their typical data-codes. "The fields are fallow today." Store, next. "I've placed my banana on the shelf." And another. "I believe the child ran that way." Click, store, transport. Her day passes in a flash before my eyes, reminding me that I am out of time. That day's final series of data-codes spring into view, labeled in large letters with **FINAL**. She—I—stare at the words, or perhaps at the data, or perhaps the difference. I cannot decipher the english of the codes this time. I did   but quickly left
my understanding. I was shocked and I'll put my shock in the public record.

The scenes I disremember are written in standard english. These scenes, it seems, occupy the break between the word and the data, the moment prior to the sentencing but after the full stop. The woman appears to see this place. I only know that she is seeing it because I know what I am not seeing, a sensation itself frightening enough to send me shaking. She shakes with me. We move in rhythm and I feel her eyes burning and now, mine, too.

The room liquifies and then reconstitutes. Relief for my eyes and hers. Now she is on her way out a door I had not noticed before, whole body vibrating so violently that her fingers bang several times against the door handle before she is able to grasp it. A warning bell loosens from the walls in response to her loss of bodily control.

> The woman opens the door.
> The woman opens th
> The woman exits her room.[5]

She enters a hallway entirely featureless but for a series of identical doors that line each side. From my perspective, I can see a steady stream of Citizens walking single-file in each direction as if themselves a pair of tracks. Their pupils do not move when they are handed new streetclothes, nor when they change. I do not see them change. No Citizen can be seen naked, except by RSCH, for whom heorshe is each already naked, that is, transparent, that is, Known.

And toward each other, there is no impetus to look. Citizens are invisible to one another while on the job, thanks to a feature of the AR contacts. Thanks to geo-locational tracking, invisibilization of others at work has become so precise, the transition between work and non-work so seamless, that I always had the impression that my own guardians simply forgot other Citizens existed while there. When data workers pass each other by, the contacts leave a small cut-out where the other Citizen was. In its place, the memory   of the space before they entered.

The woman turns abruptly to a door at her left.

----

5   And in a beneath of data.

And in a coded public record.

And in a sentence-coated coded goaded document.

And in fragmented   and in outside   an d
incomplete

She enters a room   I cannot see.

She speaks RSCH, a definite form   a face fuzzed unrecognizable and a heavy voice which was not at all a voice but more a Word.

RSCH: And can you tell me what you saw between [21:46] and [27:16]?

: I saw nothing.

RSCH: Nothing. The screen was black.

: I mean I saw the black screen. I'm sorry for mis-speaking. I saw the black screen but saw no data.

RSCH: And what do you usually see while moving data?

: I forget. When I go to the hall and into the usual spot, not this one but the one across the way, I forget and then I go home.

RSCH: Something is different this time, isn't it? What do you remember right now?

: I've no words for it.

RSCH: Think logically. Use Reason. Would we ever do something that you couldn't even put a name to? You know we have progressed so as to avoid this very un-knowable thing. Every experience can be found in the manual.

: That was not in the manual. I can't even think about it without hurting. I'm hurting. I'm herding— I don't know what's happening, the back of my neck—I don't know what it is, it feels electric....something's broken back there. I'm so sorry. I'm so sorry—I didn't do anything. I don't want my body to do this. Please believe me. Please, just look at my neck. I didn't do anything, it's just...I know I should have been in con-trol, just give me a chance. Just help me, please, I'll forget, just give me time—

Because each Citizen was patented upon invention, genetic material filed away and meticulously documented, there was always the possibility that one of us would be replaced by another identical self. None would know it, just as we cannot know anything, we can only follow the RSCH. RSCH would know we were a new-yet-identical self and thus we would be so, just as I became deviant upon my naming.

But cloning was Impure; it violates a collective duty to transcend the body by duplicating it. The patenting was a simple matter of intellectual property.

These protective measures sat at the core of all RSCH mandates, including laws regulating nutrition, hydration, bathing, and movement. In exchange for living in an era and space of heretofore impossible wellness and security, we attended to our health by living RSCH law, avoiding pathology and expelling contagion. Oldworld crises were no more, because the crises are detected   defected   before they come to be so.

Every Uncitizen was a tiny crisis to be managed, a tiny awry the path. First cut into pieces, then identified and reincorporated. The axe made the first cut. The differential   diagnosis made the rest.

And yet. I underthink. Awry the path because without awry, what might path. What is RSCH if not to make truth out of me. Is there RSCH without falsehood. Is there RSCH without me   the undertwin

JPLT

        Half-dream
        injection
      X3204902200324

    ..   ..

    .

m enacing   blankness
now

      periodically permitted to venture
      from my room into the hall, long
      as I wore proper footwear
      tethered to the walking-walls

      so close that my spare arm—hanging
      my oily skin by thread; the blue
      our loosening thing—
      each right footstep
      half-dreamt

They found out about the pain and gave me an injection. No, they found out
about my brain and set about recovering.   No, they found I
Was multiplying in my head.   **You are a bad girl.**
                                                      Resist the thoughts
                                 why   are you doing this to yourself
                                                      to goodself recover-
away   Just an injection   I did not need to see its color.

[If I gathered all the blue I would have something much larger than the
body that I feel it in.
The blue would be a tunnel collecting I   and   RSCH   at   the   other
end&there   are we   blue and red   prepositions
         pre-positioning   the other]

After a period of time in RSCH, one must either recover or rot. I must either begin the process of **Citizenship and Re-Integration (CRI)** or be abjected. I cannot ask to be abjected because the abject have always been intrinsically abject and thus unable to make requests of RSCH, who, in their benevolence, choose to model wellness even for those who exist against the future. Thus I decide upon Citizenship and Re-Integration to stave off the waiting abjective blow, set to strike upon my relapse.

I recall the intake exam, relieved to have this piece of memory back but still confused as to where it had gone. During the exam, the footsteps were not   the footsteps were real, RSCH made them so, and yet no body made them. Meanwhile, the RSCH bodies surveilled on silence, out of time with the stepping machine. I tighten my hold on this memory, Reya. Their name, Reya. Their unname I refuse to forget.

I put the memory away upon seeing a blurred dr at the foot of my bed. He says, "Today is a new day." I have not had a new day since I defected to the wild. Now I'm back in the time-keeping, and I know my CRI is about to begin.

My first re-integrative task is a dry run.

The room shifts.

Instead of the axe I hold an unassuming cylinder. Suddenly, everything around me is green, and I am at the head of a long and undulating hill. I cannot see the bottom, nor do I know if there is one. The distance is made of fog alone.

Understanding what I must do and yet unable to begin, I freeze. I feel my legs as they betray me to the ground. I jerk upward in what I now know to be *moments*, tightening my grip on the cylinder. I begin to run of someone's accord. My feet ache from disuse.

Here is the truth: I am running toward a figure. Is it   it is. All I want to do is shout at them, tell them to disappear before it is too late. I feel a weight in my right hand but can not bear to look. I am holding something or everything. I am making the price that happened to me. I was going to kill them, or re-kill them, or obliterate them. And I would not remember. And the past would tense around me spew me up into recovery like a future-making fountain. No Reya. Reya was no name, a disappearance now made unflesh. Every iteration, gone, by the swing of my cylinder.

Everything is so green, as if in myth, that is, in the oldworld, before

History. In some ways, this self, too, is before History, that is, the waiting space before my history restarts, measured in days and moments like the real thing. Even as it blurred around me, I knew I was running amid hulking trees, feet trampling yellow-toned weeds—though, because RSCH offered them, perhaps they were flowers. I could not Imagine the taste.

Their hairy two-crutched body approached my flying landscape. They seemed in that moment a stranger, growing only stranger as I watched them. They sprouted legs. Two. They grew another stomach while the first shrunk and shriveled. Their body grew concave yet remained standing, collapsing into its own bones. They grew an arm dripping blood.

Reya had turned to a beast before me. Its body swung as it moved, lilting between two of itself: the legged and unlegged; the beast and the Reya.

Is this I in the eyes of RSCH or in the eyes of myself. Is this the Reya I have been taught. These are not questions   I can answer as I pilot down the hill, nearly tripping over my feet as I run. I should I shout their name and cannot understand what I read. When my arm raises the cylinder I try to place the strike strategic and only get my beast.

I fail.

> **I LOVWHAT IS THERE YOUR BODY NOT TO K**
> **E**ya forgive me i am too Li**TERAL I DO NOT**
>   **RANSACK THE BODY I   A N N I H I -**
> LATE   i saw you told me   forgive but they
> have t**aken this   INTO A SWORD AND THEY**
> **HAVE TOLD IT HOW TO** RUN AND   I   SIT
> SPEAKING IN THE DARK   VOICE   IN
> FOUL TONES   **A GHOST A WRECK**
> **OF THIS AND I WILL BE WHOLE WITH**

My body twists like opposing sides of a knot, fraying against itself. I let go of my weapon. The would-be victim, who now only looks like Reya, holds it instead. I bare my neck.

11. The Imagination in its full glory.

The Imagination in its full glory was said to contain all of history, every thought and thing and future. Accessible at its fullest only to RSCH, the database held in it every Truth ever made, every discreditation of Untruth (each of which was itself a truth). In exchange for compliance, RSCH graciously granted us access to the part known as the Public Imagination. All knowledge that could be conceived of, every word of it, was stored both as text and as image in the Imagination. This made it easy to know precisely what we referred to with our daily english. If one said "house," we could confirm the nature of the house by searching for it: four whitewalls, two stories total, a luscious yard of NewGrass, an entrance affixed with the necessary sensors.

(The Imagination had no entry
on itself.)

Sometimes I pretended the Imagination was a person. Sometimes, beneath my thoughts, I considered the Imagination a deviant, there to make RSCH easier to read. Maybe the Imagination is like me, a Citizen who was not a Citizen, a Citizen who couldn't do it anymore. These thoughts slipped out of me like puddles, perhaps back to the source. What source? Where? What database? The Imagination could not Imagine itself and so all thoughts of it were stowed somewhere underground alongside the rest of the useless data. RSCH builds with it. Makes ourselves useful.

Use of the Imagination is not permitted to patients. We cannot be trusted to Imagine appropriately, nor are we to be trusted with access to text. Patience means being written of, taken in the language of MA, deviance, and other tongues to be dr'd, not selfed. This was part of how Reya became Reya. They could not be the dr   'd text. They did not want to be, but they also could not be, because being the text is having been by RSCH written.

We are not RSCH because we are bodies, text. We are text because we are codes RSCH has written. We are deviant when we disobey the codes. We are deviant in the manner with which we do not obey the manner. I am hungry for the end   of circular truths. I cannot believe I am thinking

    this. I am hungry for the edge or the end of this prism.

    Back in the forest, Reya framed deviance as a duty. We were, so Citizens knew they weren't. Citizens could be monitored and cared-for. Their contact-recorded memories were sorted and stored in files for RSCH review, making history   in orderly rows. One day, the Citizens would be made of memory alone, transcending the bodies that could not be trusted to store them. Deviants were outside History and outside memory. We made inside possible. We kept it in, a wild wor l dless wall.

    RSCH birthed us Pure, but when we were Impure, we had always been. As if RSCH made the dirt it shucked. As if RSCH itself made all its objects.

    Blue enters. I'm nearly viole   n   t

Do you know why you're here.

I'm Impure.

    [I'm underneath myself, doing double-duty: to say the words, to convince the top of me to believe enough to be believable]

Yes, and why else?

[MUTED]

Because you cannot be trusted.

    Do you understand that we are trying to help you because you cannot be trusted on your own? Do you understand we have shut down these thought patterns because they are terminally deviant? Do you understand that we want to keep you safe?

The words "cannot be trusted" grew, dilated, and flattened, all rimmed in blue, mostly purple.

    I AM MORE TRUSTWORTHY THAN YOUR COWARDLY CITIZENS AS I MAKE MYSELF ALONE

    By saying this I do MA behaviors. Textbook, I overhear. Then words grow   blurred as faces. The opaque table at the base of my thoughts, upturned. I try to cover it with my body but I cannot. My quiet turns to evidence. My   bared all for the common-good.

      I notice in the haze the drs jump away from me, hands raised. They slowly return. It happens again. I'm bared, but RSCH will not see me naked. RSCH was afraid of me naked. RSCH desires the unnaked without permitting for my body.

[Desire is the other side of fear.]

Antilude (Reya)

REPORT: AUTH_0204

ON [SUB. 77]

1. Subject swallowed capsules of   which neutralized the effects of   and performed illucidity when required but was in fact in a state of consciousness during the   and   .

2. Subject was to be administered nutritional shakes six times daily, began refusal, was to return to injections.

3. Was subdued. Was administered   .

4. Returned to consciousness.

5. Legs were numbed and iced.

6.   was administered in leg B for   hr &   m i n . Leg A was administered to likewise.

7. Unknown blank entered subject's cell. Following are notes from that day's recording:

    great black circle enters seemingly out of nowhere. [camera blanks] subject in unknown state, most likely semi-conscious. After entering, black circle removes large tool from side. Appears to be   units by   units; rectangular. Descends upon subject. Moves toward   a n d removes tag from   subject

MMMMmmMmmm

Oooo0000000 R QEA   RL   SKLA
                         483942002
                         04444444ERR

ERR

ERR

ERR

ERR

ERR

ERR

ERR

THIS IS REYA

CAN   YOU   HEAR
ME
CAN YOU HEAR
CAN YOU

HERE

E

R

R
\
E
R
R

I am still   stuck to the idea of my legs, the idea
that this lack of them is the thing that hurt   not RSCH and
their   their   I am gritting my teeth. I am going to say
it   say   the word now. I'm going to say the word t
tt   tor t   that one. I'm going to say that word like I mean it
someday   but right now   too easy blame my legs because
my body is used   to the blame. It has taken the blame for
the circumstances of its birth
 for all that it endured
and now, finally, for dismembering itself, even though my legs
did not simply walk away.
It was never about the flesh of them.
It was about the power to take it.
It was the power not to kill   but take. The axe, re
placing name

The Operator looks at me to tell me we don't have much time.
It tells me with its hands for eyes. Its lips form one thin ghostly
line. Its body hunches as if in the midst of a procedure, and we
are. Preceding. Proceeding. Down the same as always path but
now it is all new, because the story we seek is new. Now. The
story we seek is now

halfway-ghosting down the hall, I arrive to emptiness that knows
me. I walk further. The hall swallows me into another space and
time, tilting me amid a sea of tiny   dots my scattered vision. I am suddenly small and enhanded by drs. They
multiply euphorically. They are all hands and always faceless
and I fold   beneath their weight
I am my greatest fear   now
to be small again

> *I look down at myself and see all that they did. Save the data.*
> *Check it there. See the tag. Watch them place the metal chip. I*

see the things they left on me. I see the marks.[6]

Watch them take as if alien to my own pain. Until the pain turns you insight out   until you're running before you can decide to run and the Operator follows, back in the empty hall, back in the hall now empty of the memory you've retrieved, the hall maybe-conjured by the chip, its hypnosis, its interneck gaze.

01101000 01100101 01110010 01100101 00100000 01100001
01110010 01100101 00100000 01111001 01101111 01110101
00100000 01101000 01100001 01110110 01100101 00100000
01100110 01101111 01110010 01100111 01101111 01110100
01110100 01100101 01101110
01100101 01101101 01110000 01110100 01111001 00100000
01100010 01101001 01101110 00001101 00001010 00101101
00100000 00101101 00001101 00001010 01101110 01101111
01110100 00100000 01100110 01101111 01110101 01101110
0110010

END ANTILUDE

They find me weak and forgetting tomorrow. I can hardly keep my eyes open, but through my slits I see a silhouette. I know instantly; like the moss, their impression holds its shape. Their long-spindled crutches embolden against RSCH.

I know better than to trust what I see. As a patient all I experience is not experience until RSCH says. When it is mine it is only intuition—sworn enemy of Reason.

In the final conflict before the closing of the Community, Reason battled intuition. Reason was RSCH, won.

The room is quiet, just me and Reya's dark shape in the far corner. They move toward me. I reach out an arm I realize is connected to my blue; the needle snags my skin.

I begin to ask the obvious *how*. They speak before I do. Their hair has grown since I last saw it. Thick, yellowish bruises dot their arms and thighs, interspersed with fresh, jagged scrapes.

"I climbed in. Got messed up doing it, but I climbed in. The Operator came, looking for better tools, I think, though I'm not sure how it could use RSCH on anyone. Considering what they've done…" Reya shook their head violently and murmured something to themself.

"But the barriers? The walls?" I have no idea how high I am on RSCH's impossible wall, only that I am part of something that did not have an end.

"It's no-Citizen's land. I made…I think I made a little pocket, a dent. There's no word for it. Like—you remember. But there's no word."

Do I remember? I archive through myself. I carve quickly. I see an edge as if another silhouette, but this one flees. My memory is nothing but a series of flights, now, all moving too quickly to grab.

"The Imagination doesn't work here, anyway, unless you're a dr," I say.

"I'm not talking about the Imagination. I don't know what I did, but somewhere, there was an opening, and I passed through myself to get it, and I got bruised, and I'm here. It all felt like untying a trick. The chip helped, I think—I made me into two echoes and split them and then came back together, here, on the data base," Reya replies.

They show me the red, slimy skin surrounding their chip. I've never seen it so enraged.

The moment I squint at their angry chip, the room turns blue. I see two ghosts of Reya before me, one holding an axe, ready to swing. They swing and I only feel the echo of pain. The scene rewinds. In the blue-white light I rep   (l)   ay.

Their ghost begins to fade after the second swing. I widen my eyes to see history settling back into itself, Reya's possible embedding Reya's now. Their hands reach for my neck, feel around behind me for a chip. None.

I knew there was nothing there. My memory slipped otherwise. I watch Reya's face as their hand traces the back of my neck, how now, when I squint, they do not turn violent but ugly. Not in image, but in word itself, writ and past   ed across their body Ugly. Sick. Deviant. Contagious. A harsh dark mark to rid; my blue halo and their Other.

Turning from my neck to the blue tubes around me, from those to the needle in my arm, and from there to the doorless space through which they entered, Reya asks, "So. Where are they." They let it deflate midway into a stop.

"They could be just behind that wall." At the edges of my re-collection I locate the mirror scene. Someone, watching, through a mirror that was not at all a mirror but instead a lens.

"Do you think they are?"

"I can't think, you know that."

"That isn't what I meant and you…" Reya pauses, swallowing their know. "And… the drs behind the mirror Know that!"

"Well, now that you said it, they can't be, right, because you think lies, including but not limited to: delusions, paranoiac sentiments, ahistories…"

Soon we're both laughing, unregulated and whole-bodied. Reya perched themself at the edge of my bed; we both startled at the feel of their weight against the mattress. They were thin and hollowed like a sleeping tree, like a rejected   forest. I laughed until the shaking of my flesh, which bled from my bones in rolling hunks, distracted me. My thoughts turn blue and swift.

The past tenses me.

When I return, Reya is pulling me from the bed. The windowless walls and now-dangling tubes shake, I flail like a sack when they try to move me. The Operator enters, pulling, too. I can feel its eyes blink against my skin.

And then I'm standing.

Reya and I are eye to eye.

The Operator looses itself behind us, gathering vials of blue, gripping in sight the measuring table I could only see in edges. Its skin-pockets, normally full of operative tools, bulge with color. Bulbous indigo. Slender teal. As the Operator moves, RSCH tools clatter to the floor. It pushes them all to the violent white below its feet, throwing open the doors of cabinets I did not exist before and emptying them of tools.

Their splayed bodies made a forest of the ground.

A wild
    an unbidden site.
    A wild to un to be for
    bidden. A hole outside the thing
    ing thought.

A space |on the| out-side of sight.

Again.
    A pause appears.
    Tools make floors.
    As drops
    make doors.

The sun was thick, the ozone thin. There was little time to waste. RSCH was determined to conquer, to safeguard against, the certain death of progress. L.D. Summus, RSCH co-founder, made us survival. We would live inside a protective space through which the sun turned into energy. Thus, it became light, and light enlivened. Light became everywhere. The boundaries slowly formed.

Deviants deviated. RSCH and their sympALLIES' concerns grew amid protests both of nutrition shakes and of the psycho-logically-stabilizing drugs within them, chose more drastic ways to transgress.

Some began eating more. They catalogued their excess mass away from RSCH sight, stealing more of themselves than RSCH had permitted, carrying superfluous body mass. Others stopped eating. Women lost their breasts and thus their evidence. Yet unpatented yet still, always, and already the property of RSCH, this was an act of theft. This period of history is known as Mass Starvation, in which starvation

> Or food deprivation, which RSCH used as a method of purifying those with su-perfluous mass, but did not use, bc RSCH can only well and cannot starve.

was the form of deviance employed to strip from RSCH the matter that they rightly bore.

These were the last years of roads and sidewalks. The old deviants wore no clothing, or clothing that was purposefully so-cially-disruptive. They projected tele-signs from their primitive AR devices, such as "THINK ME WEAK / BUT I AM POWER". Like their bodies, they deviantly grammared.

Others stole the last of the non-shake nourishment, all chemically-contaminated. They ended up in the forest floor. Their toxins wrecked the soil. The wild became forbidden. Still more ate.

RSCH made many truths in this period. Regular examinations by author   ized drs began. Social Abandonment Disorder (SAD) was discovered and typified. Patients presented most obviously in their defection from the now-forming Community. RSCH expanded the description female symptomology of MA to include bodily-nutritional disobedience, paranoia / fear of persecution, distrust of authority, et cetera.

From school and from work, suspected women were loaded out back doors and onto transportational equipment to see RSCH. RSCH was a body   sloughing its dead   s k i n and growing new arms every day. What is the head? We are RSCH's mouth.

I dreamt I was in the Imagination, but it was constructed entirely of real buildings, vulgar oldworld ones. My consciousness floated down a pinkish street that seemed to wish for whiteness. A red washed of its blood. There was no sky, but there was light.

There were people in the street, gathering. They spoke to one another in various unknown englishes. When they noticed me, they turned to me as if one great mass. Their bodies reconfigured, forming a pyramid. It was as if each person's was pulled by a tall string whose holder was a mystery. They held each other up, head to foot to head. I watched, silent, as they moved into several formations, always pyramidal but varying in height and width.

The pyramids began with joy, makers smiling. Later their faces grew morbid, their new composite shapes leering, leaning at me. Each face was writ in ugly.

12. I grew   afraid.

Before Reya arrived, I grew   afraid. Afraid to become big enough, whole enough to stick me to the bed for good. Afraid that the much of me now would entirely displace the freedom I'd been, if it were freedom. Even when I'd axe, I thought, I'd bring the whole bed with me. I'd carry it on my big back. I'd be stuck there with my body and my bed, not sure where one started   where one **STOPped** and know only   the weighty mine. I could not take the growing fact of my body   anywhere, so I left it above when the blue took me into memory. I pretended I was the memory I, the hollow I, the one unfilled with RSCH.

How much of recovering, I wondered, was just carrying the bed on my back. The bed is the extra weight, the watching you watch until you are the watcher, the inside-eyes that followed all the CLASS-II ghosts I ever saw. I remembered them up when I could, even as they began to vanish. I brought them closer. I left grudging erasures where the images left. I am writing out of forgetting. I am writing out of a body remade by RSCH eyes, leaving   a public record somewhere far from bed.

The shakes became harder to manage. **You are experiencing an inappropriate reaction to nutrition administration.** Was I drinking now or later? My body sunk. My limbs loosened. My stomach dropped. Second stomach tender after RSCH tests, I fell deeper into cavernous white with each passing   of my sentence. Every word I watched them write embedded me further. I became a wall of text. There was no future; there was no past. There was deviance and there was recovery. There was my patience, placing me out of time and space, a watcher of absent clocks. All of me was known before I knew it.

Meanwhile, somehow, reintegration continued. I received notice when it came time to challenge my Uncitizening, a mandatory step of the reintegration process. I would stand before RSCH and attempt to prove myself. If I proved factual, I would move forward to more axe-trainings and

Recitizenship classes. If not, I'd return to the sinking bed. There was no practice-time beforehand because I had not yet qualified for before and after. There was no practice at all, because if I had attained access to Truth, I would truth myself naturally.

The halls were as long and white as my room, though this time I could see the floor. A speck in the pale, I struggled to walk, remembered and swallowed the *atrophy*. My spare arm dragged and screeched along the floor. My second stomach dangled. I was attached to the wall by an invisible cord. The further I walked, the more familiar each endless hall became, as if they were all one single stretch.

The hall ended when a door appeared before me. It swallowed me hole. I heard indeterminate sounds just beyond that seemed to fade with my conscious acknowledgement. I was in the center of a pit. I could only see a dangling spotlight above me, which illuminated a small circle at my feet. Still attached to my leash, I could not leave the circle. I could not enter the dark surrounding me for fear of taint. Somewhere beyond, I assumed, sat RSCH. Somewhere beyond sat a space of light, a gap, from which RSCH pierced the dark to catch me.

At first I was asked no questions. My story floated out of me in pale fluttering clouds, turning into nonsense shapes, fading from my spotlight to the darkness. My head was the stage   of recovery   u p o n which I stood. I watched my thoughts empty. Erasures
their place. Words fled until my body alone was left to observe.

"I'm here," I heard words say, "to reapply to join the the body of Knowledge. I hereby submit to wellness-review—"

My thoughts continued loosening like smoke. I shivered. I tried to speak, but faced immediate re-covering. Why, here, was my story telling without my mouth? The thought made me jump. One of my born-arms flew to my now-covered mouth. Before I knew what I was doing, I was uncovering. I opened like a wound.

SUBJECT SENSES UNREALITY. DETECTED. RE-SUB-STANTIATE REALITY IN 5, 4, 3—

My muzzle confused around my mouth. A white-hot flash momentarily lit the entire area, but what I saw was so quickly stripped from my memory that I may not have seen it at all. My arm was frozen near my still-uncovered face. I was unfrozen. I wiggled my fingers, grasping one smoky thought.

SUBJECT IS FROZEN. RE-ALERT REALITY IN—

I heard my memories as told in a voice that was not my voice, but higher, like a siren. This was the same voice that had submitted to assessment. It was a voice spoken by a woman with a name. Her name—my hand froze again. The thought slipped from between my fingers.

The woman speaks again. "I am here to defend myself. I'm here to tell you that I have the ability to self-regulate so as not to require RSCH's imposition of captivity and subjecthood —»

ON WHAT GROUNDS

A different voice identical in tone asked

AND WHAT TRUST SHALL WE HAVE IN YOU, WHOSE MIND IS MOTTLED BY YOUR DEFECTIVITY, TO MAKE CLAIMS ABOUT THE STATE OF YOUR SUBJECTHOOD

A trap. I could not tell her. I hardly knew her. I remembered I knew nothing at all. This new woman was the difference between me and the muzzle.

She spoke in a different voice this time, one similar to my own. "I live in here," **she said of her worthless anti-mind.**

My frozen body began to crumble. First my toes and fingers, then my wrists and ankles. I lightened as my organs stripped. A RSCH voice continued

SUBJECT LACKS INSIGHT

I tried to yell. Because I live here. BECAUSE I LIVE

SUBJECT LACKS SUBJECT LACKS INSIGHT LACKING INSIGHT SUBJECT LACKS INSIGHT SUBJECT LACKS IN SITE SUBJECT LACKING IN SIGHT SUBJECTED LACKING SIGHT SUBJECT

They then began to say it in a way I no longer recognized, in a way I was not intended to understand. It was another english entirely, garbled as if through liquid. I saw blue in front of my eyeballs, drowning my pupils. My mind turned its color. My neck snapped.

No matter where I turned, my back was to someone. There is always that weakness in our necks. That spot   like RSCH   l i g h t we cannot see from dark, words in englishes too Pure to understand.

REPORT: TESTER_AR_SMARTFILE™_MEMO

IF YOU HAVE CREATED MEMORIES WITH SMARTFILE™ TECHNOLOGY, PLEASE REGISTER YOUR MEMORY FILES WITH THE APPROPRIATE RSCH BANK. ANY MEMORY MADE OR MODIFIED WITH SMARTFILE™ TECHNOLOGY IS THE PROPERTY OF RSCH AND MAY BE SUBJECT TO FURTHER STUDY.[7]

---

7 Draft to be reviewed by disseminatory officials on   after completion of trial period on   OR once supply of   has liquidated.

My second stomach was made up of delicately interconnected tubes, whose corresponding holes in my sides were perpetually sore from the disturbance. Never entirely healed, like the rest of me,

Healing was for RSCH alone.

every hole was read as surrounded by sores. All red, all oozing just-slightly, the irritation became my body itself. My body was indeed an irritant. A scratch at RSCH's side, a bellow in my own. I could not think myself in the body. I was the mind, as RSCH said, and I sought to transcend. I knew I could not continue forever believing both in and out of RSCH, but I had no other frame for looking. A body was a body was a despicable body and it was painful enough to knock my blood-walled edges.

My tubes stretched from the second-stomach itself—a fleshy, pulsing bag—up through my esophagus. The tube sat at the back of my throat such that I was always gagging. I could choose when to digest and when to reject, and when I rejected, the tube-bound food slid from my throat and into the attachment at my waste. My waist   heavied with it. The fleshy compartment itself was composed of the scraps from my chest, two bulbous bags stitched together and fashioned to my side. One used-to nipple had become my stomach's emptying point. The other, penetrated at its center by the esophageal tube, became an entrance.

It was one of the few pieces of me I permitted to be thick, pink, puckered, and soft. I did not attempt to change it, for the pink-puckering was the simple fact of the stomach's existence. So, too, the spillage: my second stomach's emptying-hole leaked whenever I walked. The earth was plagued by my fluids. In the moments I stopped to empty the thing, I made a hole, a third stomach, and graved the substance my leaks had only hinted at.

The burial became a ritual, a form of compulsive behavior which **holds the mind, disturbs well-thoughts, and distracts from the duties of Citizenship**. First I would remove my garment entirely. I would walk slowly toward the passing river, at the banks of which I'd dig my hole. I would dig deep enough to find damp dirt both in the hole and beneath my fingernails, and I would evidence the hole until empty. Then I would wade into the water and step on my reflection, again and again and again, until it was as if I'd trodden myself two-dimensional. Like a screen. Like a line of data. Like the very RSCH from which I stole myself, only to remake an

Order into me. I realized in these river-moments that I had not defected. That all I was was RSCH, too, Community or wild, frontside or ba

I had first asked the Operator only to cut out my first stomach. It refused, explaining that this would kill me. I begged. It told me it had preserved the breasts, showing me their remnants in a murky jar. It had an idea for how to use them.

It hollowed a fleshy chunk from my abdomen to make room. I didn't think I'd care, but after it was over found myself crying not at the pain but at its opposite, loss. Absence. How much of me could disappear before I was someone else? Would I know it? Would I,   gain a different name? Or would I melt into the soil with the rest of me, no longer a me at all but simply pollution, uncountable?

The physical pain was bad. It always was. I have no more words to explain the physical pain because there are none in english. When Reya found me after the procedure, laying beside my bloody chunk, they buried it themself. They didn't ask me how I felt. They could not think too closely to the operations, for fear of chip-activation.

We had tried it once before, together, installing crude magnets in our fingertips like the old modders did. Reya's chip went on soon after we'd finished, hands a bloody mess, bites of flesh all scattered at their crutches and my feet. They fell hard onto the finger-pieces and did not leave the spot until the following day.

The Operator didn't watch us put in the magnets, and as a result, we both damaged our nerves. This was fitting, even funny, because the nervous system accounted for the overwhelming majority of deviance cases recorded by RSCH. The whole area got infected, spurting yellow fluid until the fluid turned clear. I was still new to the wild, then, new enough to be disgusted by my seeping body. I didn't yet understand the way my fluid could water the earth. I learned slowly as I turned to RSCH—braced *against* RSCH as if pushing a wall—that the pollution could be duty. I could water the wild. I began to run with my fingertips spread, remembering rain to the ground below my feet. It was disgusting and horrible and new.

We did not say that all our freedom, just like our confinement, came from RSCH. It was only the values that made us   Uncitizens that allowed us to defect. But there was nothing else, no material to fold into this space of unexpected movement. Reya did not speak the name of RSCH. So long as the name went unsaid, we, too, could run beneath saying. Otherwise, we would have no choice but to be Known.

The first time I was to empty my second stomach, we went to the river together. They waded several paces behind me, stopping once the water reached their waist.

I clutched my stomach, squeezed. I dumped myself below the water's surface. My detritus first floated, then slowly sunk. If the scraps were me, I was sending me everywhere.

"It's not going to stop." Reya said this when I finally turned around.

"The river?"

"And us." A pause, and then a hurried, "I mean, us running forever. Never being stuck in a place long enough to recognize ourselves. We're just names, always changing. They're just going to keep re—"

I am in the nonsense more and more. A ravenous living thing. I lose sight and sound, the Purest senses, most often. I retain smell so I may smell my rot. I can smell the rotten flesh amid the treeroots but can no longer find my way. In my bluened dreams

> And are they dreams, if I dream them more   than wake? Are they dreams if brought out not by sleep, but blue? Is sleep, sleep, if mandated?

They come in unpredictable flashes. I bury my face deep in Reya's stomach but my body loses touch and I am only a watcher. The shake comes. I watch our bodies haloed. The scene turns to horror, an axe striking the space between us. Our touch turns bloody before going dark. Reya sits in front of me, frozen in time, until the axe arrives. When it hits it etches at some core I cannot understand. Each time I emerge wizened. A little fewer, in pieces.

A small voice at the back of me asks after the blue. It appears

as though a small dose of the blue triggers and then dims memory, and a full dose acts as removal. Erasures come piecewise as incorporation occurs.

The voice belongs to no one I know. I wear only my own context. I am a lit background, where I do not know if I am remembering or being remembered. Our bodies turn to monsters and the stories twist and twist until I cannot dream or see or sleep or wake but only fog. I hear the remains of my name in an english that hurts, but cannot hurt, because there can be no hurting in RSCH.

Between doses I try to order myself.

My second stomach: here, near-   detached. I cannot see to check the oozing, but RSCH bears no taint

> If RSCH bears no taint, how was I born? Was Reya?

I can see my room remains white. I can still see blue in the corners of my vision. I cannot see the room's corners, if it possesses corners. I discipline my pulse, attempting not to alert drs to my efforts.

No one has spoken to me since the review. drs wear protection from my attempts at english. drs hear   heal real things. My voice I am dispatching in is unreal, and my underspeaking makes it so. I am not real, I remind myself. My wild untime slips into their hands as fileable memory, yet as it does, it pushes into RSCH Truth.

There is a rustle in the walls somewhere. The rustle tells me the walls exist, though I see only an expanse of white. I wait for the dream voice to come back, but it does not. The rustle continues and I believe I see a soft yellow dot the whiteness in front of me, though as soon as I realize, the yellow is gone. The room and I are skinless once again.

In a version, I was axer. I saw real blood. In a version, I confronted them. In a version, I do not know who *them* is, or are. In a version Reya saved me and we fought and won. Perhaps this last version was not a saving, though, because we are unsalvageable. In that version, Reya stole me from saving. Each time I tumbled foot over foot through the forest, trampling remnants a I ran, hitting metal and bones like pebbles in the dirt.

In this version, I saw the Operator in the distance. It prepared its craft. Somehow, I knew the axe would not impact the Operator. I was aiming for the patient, that is, the person upon whom the Operator made marks, though only RSCH may have patients. The Operator had none because it, itself, was nothing at all. I was anxious to arrive, yet my realization of the Operator's nothingness slowed me. I briefly had no object.

At that moment, the Operator disappeared behind a tree, leaving a prostrate blue body in its wake. I kept running. When the Operator returned from the tree, it carried a long set of pliers. It dipped the pliers deep into the patient's mouth. It dipped so far I was sure that by the time I arrived the pliers would have already struck cerulean gore and perhaps exited their back.

The pliers emerge, weeping blood and other fluids, from the patient's now-gaping jaw. One by one, the Operator removed its organs. The mouth grew to size the stomach, heart, liver, kidneys, and lungs. Intestines emerged like long, rancid strings.

The blue of the body enticed me. I was close now, felt a hunger I had not before. For once I raised my blade myself. I watched myself decide it, I watched the Operator realize, hand-eyes raised to meet my own. But before I could bring the thing down, the Operator reached into the blue patient's nose, so deep I trembled, gagged, and lost track of the axe. It extracted a clear tube from one nostril. The tube was full of the color of the patient.

Several RSCH convene at my bedside. My nose gags now. My burn wraps tight around my throat. I cough and spit the blue onto my chest, which sends RSCH sirens flashing, sends boldface I cannot recall in   -com-ing. The woods looks   looked from the vantage underneath the stars. Buildings all below. Something builds inside so I erect it from my mouth until I touch the lid. Bodies walk the perimeter, each as if siphoned by tube. They are so small I could suck them up.

I begin to suck. I suck my girlhood back inside. Do not make sudden movements. Do not give cause to a summoning of the police. Do not gag the shake. Do not give cause to RSCH doubt of your sanity. Do not allow harm to come to yourself. Do not let yourself go.

The room is gone.

Again: When you receive the call, you will sprint
through the woods with some sharp object. You
do not get to see the woods. You run the margins
of the city your existence on the line. The knife
edge takes on the dark. You can feel it. I'm sorry,
dark. You continue   running—how
many times have you sent this? You are already
running for your whole life. You are made of
your life spent running. You cannot face your axe.
You cannot blood your knife. You draw the body

you are made to draw. The ring of the axe makes the body into black and
white and the black and

white reads Citizen and Citizen
          you be   come

13. Time passes. From a place

Time passes. From a place between dreaming and death, I can look at Reya and see someone new, transformed by what I've learned. Bodies become babies anew when we learn new things to see them. Reya's lips move above me, but I hear nothing between them. I blink once more and my hearing gathers.

"Hey   Where did you go? Can you tell me your name? Can you remember who you are?" The questions make me anxious, an emotion I haven't felt in earnest since before all this. I am back with Reya. I can sense their concern and hate it as much as this question. What was my name? Why did it matter? What would it do to me, to be called it, and would I recognize the call at all? To know my RSCH name would only summon them, I realize, rouse the drs. We only realize our spaces in the absence of calling.

"It can stay lost," I say of my name.

"It could, if it were simply missing," they answer. "But it isn't. It was taken. Just like—" they stop. I think about the *not about the legs*. It's not about my name. It's about the not-minehood, the act of taking which is not taking because it was never a question of possession, but borrow a loan   a l o n e life of borrowed time.

"I've lost a lot more. I don't need a name," I say. My born-limbs are weak yet swollen, my attached-limbs near-collapse. Pale and mottled and inexplicably damp, my spare arm is scrawny whereas the rest of me has plumped.

"Seems like you're gaining them, too," they say, gesturing at the rest of my body, smiling a toothy vine-twist smile. Though I wear the same garment I have worn since the start, my sleeves no longer come to a sharp point perpendicular to my shoulders. They close like tiny mouths around my upper arms, leave small re a d lines against my skin. A plushscape of white, glossy strings crawl from my armpit to my inner-elbow.

I scowl. I contain so much of RSCH now, my center packed with their gaze like tight wads of—of what? Whatever   it was

A battle

It was a battle for my body between RSCH and myself, each bent on cleansing me of the other, yet needing the other in order to stay alive.

Surely, this underknowledge is a gained-thing, too. I have gained the ability to think it without **STOPping**, to under think the RSCH real. I say these sentences to myself so I do not push past Reya   excavate

for   the floor a flesh pile of—   **STOP**

Reya squeezes me just a little. Here were all the hauntings I had never truly unthought.

"In some ways," I concede. I press against my limits. I cannot Imagine. I under think ways of disappearing myself. I fail.

"But not your name back."

"It wasn't ever mine. You know that. Anyway, did you even get your name back, after the second time?"

"The first time, I was… *he* was young," Reya speaks of the other person, the little boy. I tilt my glass to better their vision. "He was discharged with his name. You only get your name if you're well enough to speak yourself, otherwise, they reassign it. He brought RSCH with him wherever I went. It wasn't ever okay, but it happened for a while. He got out by not getting out. But the second time? I had to leave him there with that name, the legs. I had to leave him behind to make sure they couldn't see me. Otherwise, they would have caught me before I started. I knew that. You know that. They have my legs as evidence already. Whenever I try to remember it big enough to see, the chip—" they shook the possibility from their head. There is a RSCH patent on every real name, ensuring every Citizen had a unique and legitimate identifier. I never knew how Reya could be made from nothing at all, its substance outside the question of naming and wholly unpatented.

"Is that how you got back in, too, with *Reya*?"

They gained the tile floor with the end of their crutch, contaminating, contemplating, leaving tiny broken pieces. I realized couldn't remember what they went by in school, or if they went by. At the time it all seemed so nothing compared to the more immediate fears, weights and measures and other vital things bookended by work, memorizing and recording and learning how to pace   myself. How could they have attended

school under that name and not have been caught? (Because it was not
a name) Without the contacts? (Unreal, they had no eyes) They should have
been shunned, student duly monitored for Inappropriate & Unauthorized
Self-Descriptive Behavior.

"I can't explain it," says Reya, watching my face and knowing the
holes. "I'm afraid to, anyway." We look around us. The room still appears
empty. I consider how much RSCH isn't watching   but   fear   the
watcher immanent. The steps are a recording, are a person. This record, a
body or a slippery text.

So far, time remains   unhappening. Truth has not caught up.
No drs entered our plot, not through any hole, though their eyes lived somewhere inside our own.

We exit to a dizzying hall. So long as we do not think it, there are
doors. The doors to each room, spaced exactly the same width apart from
each other and nearly blending into the shattering whiteness of the walls, are
nearly invisible. When I finally discern one, I touch it, and it clicks open to
reveal a room identical to my own. I almost see my shadow there. *Was* it my
own? Is this hole   is this whole place a memory? It all feels so easy
and so waiting.

The doors, once appeared, are too heavy for me to push open. Even
Reya, whose arms ripple with crutching-muscle, struggles against the weight.
We finally succeed when I press my body hard against one door and Reya
uses both arms and couches to heave it open. They press the front of their
body into mine, a thick touch I did not know I so needed until I felt it.

When we push, Reya stumbles, and I fall to my back. When I rise, I
hear faint sounds.

"In here," says Reya, pushing their way inside a cracked door from
which spilled fluorescent light. A boy lays prone on the bed, eyes wide open.

Reya chokes on their breath. "Seriously?" They demand, half-laugh-
ing.

The boy in front of us has green eyes. I know those eyes, wide and
watery as fresh NewGrass fresh. He's bigger now, tall and hairless.

"So I was right. They ended you," Reya says. I sit, exhausted, beside
Reya's crutches.

"I had no chance," says the green-eyed boy. "They should have told me I was no chance."

"You were no chance?" Reya tests the words in their mouth. Sadness traps in their eyes. I blink my own eyes, slowly, as if to capture it.

"I wasn't, not any chance," says the green-eyed boy in a small voice. Reya is silent. I feel something release like a trapdoor between them.

At school, the days in the immediate wake of the green-eyed boy's departure smelled different than the days before.

> I didn't ask if anyone else noticed. So much of the dance of Citizenship was not asking, saying nothing, for fear that the rest thought the way you thought a problem.

I was unsure why I was so affected by the change in smell, subtle yet, to me, impossible to ignore. Perhaps it was my hours in the elsewhere with Reya. Maybe it was because, when a body left a space, the air simply gained some new and enweightened property, a property stinking of its own unbearable emptiness, hauntsick. In class, all remained the same, and half of me feared that it was only I who noticed the smell's wet weight. If only I noticed it, it was surely my own defect—I had already, after all, defected from the collective perception. To speak such a thing aloud would worsen my case. So I kept it in, even when all its implications became so overwhelming I wanted to bury my face in my arms and remember him until the air was clean and I was no longer.

One day in the immediate wake of his going, when we were all actively **STOPping** him out of space, time, and memory. He was not and had never been, by virtue of having been and having deviated.

"A boy asked a question a few days ago," I told my mother when I could no longer bear it. She had only just come home from a day of data, was rearranging the house and snapping photos as she went, putting each of the lenses occupying each room-corner on its own timer. They could at any time be recording data for RSCH. Separately, we could take our own photos with them and upload them directly to the Network, also monitorable by RSCH.[8]

My mother made an up-chin gesture with her head, and I obediently made eye contact. I felt a linkage. She was recording.

"And," she asked.

A test I was bound to fail.

"Do you smell something? Something new?" I asked. As I said it, the smell grew stronger—unpleasant, but familiar; a bit like the edges of the wild.

"So it's true." She narrowed her eyes. She took a long sip of her

---

8 I wish I had more to say on the Network's details, but because I inked before adulthood, my experiences are shallow.

shake, and I had no idea what she meant. I had no idea we were drinking the shakes until they appeared before us. She sipped again. I took a countersip, nearly choking at the thickness, the nutty taste of brown sludge, traipsing down my throat in mid-sized globs. I remained calm. I did not allow my throat to close.

"What?" My knuckles did not whiten around my glass. My legs did not shake. My behavior was not that of one induced to panic.   Stop, stop, stop—

"I've smelled it on you."

I looked into her eyes, attempting my best Citizen-gaze. I met her eyes and it hurt. I poured into her, past the contacts whose vague outlines blotted the left side of her left eye and the right side of her right. I felt heavy, like a weight was pushing me forward and into her; I struggled not to tip over.

"Where have you been going?"

I took a tiny—toosmall—sip of the shake. I was supposed to drink as if grateful. I used my right hand to pick up my left, wrap its fingers around the glass. She was still recording. I drank again, still too small.

"I don't know what you mean," I said. "I walk to school, walk home, go with you to the milieu on errands. Where else could I be?"

The drink, in my hand, looked about to burst from the cup. I was a tight-hooked bow. I was a string to burst. I was many things without names. I wanted more than anything to have fled already, to be out
in the woods: Reya and I
and nothing t

        o hurt us

Reya and I had been together, alone, but not in the unspeakable way we were later on. It seemed that, simply, spaces stuck. People stuck and unpeople stuck worse. Dirt stuck, left a mark. This was the principle of all of it, that RSCH would unstick us from our bodies and our contagious others, cure us

     of the ills design

         at   ed by RSCH.

        ills which at their worst drove Citizens to Uncitizen, to attempt
        to annihilate themselves   their belonging, killing their bod-
        ies, venturing to the wilds, the wilds after life, beyond RSCH,
        beyond here, beyond the Community and leaving only a body,

an incomplete, diseased fossil behind—death. Outside time and outside law, though forever carrying its shadow.

I decided it was death my mother smelled on me, and that she was more afraid than I was. I gulped more of the shake, and in several swallows, it was gone. I drained the thing with an efficiency that disgusted me (a disgust I quickly **STOPped** out of concern for my heart rate). I wiped my mouth with the napkin beside me, sucking the remaining sludge from its corners, opening the napkin when I was finished. She hardly looked at it.

"There. Drink like you want to live," she said. "You know, I only do this because I want you to live. I want you to thrive. I believe in that for you. Resistance—it isn't healthy. It's stressful. It's not… natural, it's like—" (She stopped herself before "death" slipped out.) "We aren't meant to say no to life. You know that, don't you? No more of this rotten stink in my house."

She stood over me, now. She looked into the glass, whose sides were stained with brown residue.

"You left some."

"I didn't mean to." I gulped before I thought, rendering unnecessary the need to **STOP**.

"Yes," I said, remembering I was supposed to say "yes" to life. We smiled loudly at each other. Then, I retired to my room, standing in the center of the space until I felt a familiar jab of exhaustion. I stayed standing a little longer, shifting my weight from ball to toe, moving each foot in turn, eyes shut, replaying the scene in my head, wondering how long it would take to fall. I studiously avoided thinking about Reya and about the place I would go more often if not for this. Then, my knees buckled and I sank to the floor, eyes filling with tears not of sadness but out of exhaustion. I crawled to my bed, heard a small sound of confirmation once on my back.

●

"They took away my parents," says the green-eyed boy. "And the name they gave me—not my real name, it was just the name I wanted. I was copying a real man someplace else."

"How'd you get to school, with parents like that? Why didn't they get you earlier?" asks Reya. They look tall and sure above me.

"We tried to hide my... me. They did the enabling, all that, said it was like the old ones did. The deviation happened later, not right away, you know. I'm not quite like you."

"You still almost ruined everything for me, you know." Reya is toneless.

The green-eyed boy squints back at them. No words pass. The silence whitens, whitens, unfills. There is loss that was too great to be loss, a deprivation felt only indirectly at the corner of what was once full, like seeing RSCH corner by corner.

The boy weeps. I avert my eyes automatically, resisting the urge to physically recoil. Reya leans on their crutches, still expressionless. I have seen them cry before, but only as a result of the chip. They'd always feel their slick face as if their hands were strangers to it, and I would remember uncomfortably in those moments that I was the only one who had ever seen them cry; they could not see themself.

The green-eyed boy sucks in a breath and speaks through the saltwater. "In the beginning, they said if I complied I could see everything. Get my name back, my identification. None of it came. We were—" He closed his eyes. "How old were we? It doesn't matter, we were small. They laid me down one day, soon after intake. Still told me the whole time I could be finished soon if I complied. **All you need to do here is get better**, they'd say."

All of us cringe at once, hearing the voice.

"And yeah, they laid me down, and after that—after that it all got scrambled and I saw things, nothing made sense, and when I woke in between... in between administrations, you know, I asked to see my guardians. I believed they'd come and get me out."

"They couldn't even if they wanted to," says Reya. Their voice is cold, their face floor-facing.

"They wanted to," the boy says.

"How?" The idea that my guardians could or would take action against RSCH directive seemed absurd.

"My parents…"

He counts his fingers one by one, once and again and a third time. I look around, waiting for some dr to burst in, restrain his hands. Nothing came. He counts a fourth time and speaks quietly. "My parents were doing things that weren't—I don't know how to explain it. They didn't give me the words. On purpose, I mean, they didn't want me able to think it all. It was something against RSCH. Some

counterRSCH, they called it, I think. I remember the non-word but none of the filling."

I make a note of that and widen the record's gap.

He starts to cry again, and his tear-stained voice drilled holes into my skull.

"Do you have any idea where they are now?" I ask.

Through his tears, he says, "I don't even know *if* they are now. I don't know if they ever were. They could be someplace else here, how would I know?" I watch him sick   speak   sink back into himself, shrinking with his body. His eyes move in and out of focus. No more is to be done.

He nodded once at us in pointed release.

"You can come, you know," I say, unsure if coming or going.

"Not quite," he says, and his eyes unfocused once more, and together in silence Reya and I watch him shake from, and then seek   back into, consciousness.

"Just keep crying," says Reya, half-serious. "Get enough tears on the floor and you'll make this place more us than RSCH. Plenty of fluids will have to make something happen. Crumble, take all this with it."

I know RSCH needs him—us—the way we need the sun for fuel, like the mirror needs an imprint to reverse. He holds his dry, flaking body, rocking slowly. I notice my ash-chapped hands. For a moment, I imagine the three of us all leaving   ironic trails, fallen skin, tears of another kind.

Reya and I return to the hall.

"Will he ever get out?" I ask. Underneath, the question: Will *we*? And *where*?

"Out of that body? Out of here?" Reya asks. "Did I?"

They say it all into the dense nothing.

Next, we enter an administrative room, windowless and all white, subjectless without a cot or table. It looks like the office from my borrowed memory, the performance interview. All the lights are on, just as before. By one white wall is a counter topped with several foreign instruments, lined up one by one. Still no drs. The room does not look as if abandoned in haste: any invisible closets and drawers had been properly concealed before exit. The air felt heavy, though, and I feel it hang over the back of my neck like a pair of eyes.

We exit quickly. Each nearby room we enter is exactly like it, and we stay in none for more than several moments. Inside each room, I feel the same sensation: that I am not only being watched, but in the process being watched, already captured.

The line of identical empty rooms ended abruptly at another set of doors, which we push through far more easily than the last. This hallway is just like the last, lined with doors on either side, opening to more of the same.

"What are we looking for? Another—like the green-eyed boy?"

"I'm looking for my legs," says Reya impatiently, as if this were obvious. "What are *you* looking for?"

"What? Your legs? I didn't think you wanted them back."

We reach the end of the hall. Reya uses their shoulder to push open another set of doors. The rooms remain identical. It is as if the building itself is attempting to bore   into us. My eyes are heavy.

"I don't want them back," Reya says. "But I don't want to be here anymore. Not any part of me. I told you before, it's not the legs…"

"It's what they *mean*, I know. Like my name, or the name that used to be mine. But isn't that giving them what they want?"

"I want out."

There it was.

"If we get… if we get out of here, I could bury them. With every body else. And anyway, I don't care what happens after I get them back, I just want the satisfaction of holding them. I want to remember what it felt like to hold something, to have it feel like my own—and now, to have it *be* my own. My legs don't exist. They don't belong to RSCH, just like the rest of me. And anyway, don't *you* want a name, despite it all? Don't you want the satisfaction of having that back, even if you want to believe yourself stronger without it?" They continue like this, half talking-past and half in-future.

"Think about your body. You try to get rid of it, master it, make it nothing, then lose it in the process and realize that trying to foresake your name and body is really just giving both to RSCH. It's just giving up what little you have left. I don't want to have been caught that way."

I examine my body through the head-hole in my garment. I remember the hard power in my absence, which simply played the rules of RSCH slantwise.

"The only thing is to get on the other side of all of it."

We continue walking, more slowly and without any pretense of checking the rooms. What a strange thing it was, I realize, to be doing the checking—to walk freely and encounter emptiness again and again, as if I were RSCH in search of a subject.

It's the records we are   after
said Reya.
That's where they're keeping us.
I say nothing, keep this one to my heart. I depopulate my thoughts.
Then, a sound. Not the boy, nor anything recognizable.
Reya: "Did you hear that, —"
They try to end the sentence with my name. It looks like   ?"

                    ?

                ??

                        ?   .   Their
lips make strange shapes around the silence. I try unsuccessfully to understand.

> Lipreading became illegal long ago, had long ago
> been deemed unacceptable in that it enabled those
> with incorrect-sensory disorders (ISD) to revel in their
> dysfunction. Some deviants could do it, and it was use-
> ful in silently evading axers in the woods. Its illegality
> coincided with the start of the axing program.

"I remembered your name for a little while," sighs Reya. The hall
dips around us like water. "I would think it to myself, trying to keep you
around. One day—or maybe it was gradual, I don't quite remember anymore—it slipped away from me, never came back. I was afraid they'd—I
guess I didn't know how it worked for people who started off as Citizens with
real identification. Thought it might have been a sign that they just ceased
you."

Reya's voice shakes slightly, not with pain but with anger, **the most
threatening of all passions**. They bang their crutch against the RSCH
floor   once and then twice, as if daring a dr's response. The
building makes no remark at the strike. No dr comes. The silence following
the crack possessed a sonic quality all its own. In its place grows a chorus of

voices impossibly numerous and densely stacked.

"I hear it."

They grow louder slowly as we move.

"We're descending," says Reya, looking behind us. The rippling terrain rises in our wake.

We were. We dropped.

As we drop, time still

seemed not to move.

If it does, the movement a sideways

a negotiation

Deep in the woods, intoxicated by my own flight, I had initially gone a bit wild with the hormones. I was still young. Small. Trying to free my body from purity, with purity, trying to use the same old RSCH methods as if they would set me free. I wandered with all the rest to our supplier, our mystery shrouded figure, and replaced what RSCH gave me with something new. Something stolen. I became a stolen body, shrinking round its stolen substances, and temporarily, a stranger even to myself.

What did the hormones happen to me? I went off and on them and off again. They made me hungry for real things, hungry to sit beside Reya and hear what I could about their past, if that was indeed was it was, if theirs was a life or had happened at all. At the same time, my body unhappened, and every morning I woke up to discover some new part of myself: a hair, a nerve, a bit of skin; soon after, an arm, a stomach.

Reya was more ambivalent, and predicted RSCH's devastating withdrawal long before it happened. *It was only a matter of time*, they had noted, *before RSCH realized the balance was all wrong.*

What balance?

The balance between deviance—deviants—and the rest. Too many of us use the hormones now in ways we shouldn't be. They're more dangerous than advantageous when everyone using them is in the wilds.

Anyway, they said later, they didn't want any more of *that stuff* inside them. And it was hard: they had been tried on testosterone and tried themself on estrogen, but quickly grew tired of such an exhausting ritual whose every administration brought them back to the chip and its preconditions, to a shaking heap on the ground. When they got the Operator to help, it was even worse. Eventually,

> They abandoned the project, turning
> their ability to *nothing*, to love
> every second of undoing,
> antidoing—into a mod
> all its own.

At the same time, I was made flat from neck to waist, one long, reddish line from *coast-to-coast*. This was an expression Reya had heard in their past life, from another deviant before us. It meant from one side to the other, all-the-way. From one tender spot beneath one arm, to the other. The phrase made me smile. It seemed appropriate given the unnamability of whatever was happening to me—a useless expression for a nonsense body.

"But what I like most about the phrase," said Reya, "or at least, what the person who told me—I don't remember their name, only that they said they were really more than one, but in the same body, so they were *they*, and I think they thought I was, too, because I'm also they…"

Back then, Reya's ability to think off-track baffled and impressed me, too. I thought often about being *they*. There were enough of me to warrant it, though I wasn't sure what such a word would mean, considering that in truth, there were none of me at all.

"But what do you like about it, about the word—the phrase?" I pressed. *Coast-to-coast*, I thought again. Reya so easily ran off into digression, narrating themself entirely out of order. It was the sort of thing that had to be unlearned early and ideally while at school: in a childhood they hadn't ever had. But there they were, running always to the other side of language. It was simply difficult, sometimes, to understand.

"I like that even when it talks about going from one side to another, it seems like there's something else outside of it. A coast, and then what?" A coast, and then unwonderable things. The coming-after there were no words in our english to say.

I spent some time thinking about edges after that, about what it meant that RSCH had no end and yet we Uncitizens were not of it. Wouldn't we have to be part of RSCH if we were in its belly, though we ourselves were the Community's greatest enemy?

Reya poses with one hand to the wall, the other grasping around the chip-node in their neck. Their crutches had extended automatically, as always, to accommodate their arm movement, but the balance they provided was precarious at best. I hear a vague and placeless sound that I'm sure will become important later on.

"You're back," Reya says to me.

"It's coming back. I'm trying to write it back—I'm trying to fill the blue spots in. I can hear it at this depth. This one was about the mods. I remembered *coast-to-coast*. Things are filling out." I press my hands to the front of my smock, stomach flipping at the nascent blubs beneath: those shakes, I knew, contained agents to enliven my scar-flat chest.

"If there's anything in there, the Operator can take it out for you. Maybe I'll get it put in me instead," Reya says, looking at my chest, face near a smile. Their body was slack without the hormones.

"Can you see it?" I ask, examining myself again.

"Will you believe me if I tell you, before you can go up to the river and have a look yourself at what the water says?"

"You talk as if you're so sure we'll ever leave this hallway." As if I'll ever leave this body. This hallway body. This narrow   enough   to swallow. "How long has it even been since we've gone through another set of doors?"

"A while, you know I don't know. We're descending, I can feel it. See, the hall floor's turned into little tiny steps just up ahead." Steps appear several lengths from us. The hall ahead does not appear narrower, only steeper and after taking several steps forward I feel an immediate drop. Reya continues following the wall with their hands.

Then:

I feel something in the wall.

"What?" I demand, watching Reya's hands. Their skin is chalkier than before.

Reya looks me in the eye, a rare occurrence. "I didn't say anything."

"You feel something in the wall," I say. "I heard it. In a different voice, but I heard it. It was a darker voice, something like that, something a little buried."

"There some kind of mod that lets you read minds now?" Reya

laughs nervously. "Didn't think RSCH would give it to you, of all people."

"It wasn't like I read your mind, though, I just heard it as if you said it, but through a wall, or several. I think… Reya, what do you feel in the wall?"

"Give it time," Reya says.

This time I allow them the privilege of opacity with little complaint. I am sick   of transparent. Instead I watch their lips from the corner of my eyes, imagine touching them. I walk on to the feel of this image. They crutch against the wall, sneaking   peaks   all their own.

It was still unthinkable and when they put their hands and the
needles in me neon-blue
tubes thick with their fluid sheen dry   outside, to my
touch—to think about these was was from teal shade   in   a
begging   or   end

text a gerund   ing inside me   an unsure   dis- ordering   a life
if this   is a life, if this is what this is to be
something

"Where do you think they're all hiding?" I whisper to Reya, soft as if soft has ever stopped RSCH from hearing.

"I'm sure they're here. Doing their job as well as ever, it seems," Reya mock-whispers back. I remember the pre-recorded footsteps. What would a dr be doing, crouching in the corner of a basement or hallway? What would make them jump?

"—and even if not, they're close enough," continues Reya. "Or, if not—actually, it doesn't really matter if no drs are present. They're here. Right on my neck."

I shiver. It is far colder down here, as if I am entering the center of the earth. The temperature continues to drop. Slowly, the lights dim. My pace matches the sound of their crutches against the floor. I notice the darkening hall only when two shadows begin to follow us do I notice the darkening hall.

I have felt this way before.
I feel this time   I am walking too
far into it ever   come out.
And bringing   bringing and
      brining them   down with me,

I am turning us in   to a goodbye

I have felt this way before so I feel
I am not alone. I am together
with at least one other of me

STOP

My voice says
      allowed

      The tunnel stops. I try to breathe. It's purple, but it's a purple I can see, not the absent-purple that comes with staring too long into the darkness. (I'm not afraid of the darkness, I decide. But I fear the light color that darks it.)

      Now we meet a skinnier hall, a tender branch off the old descent. In a different light, I decide, the walls white, giving the illusion

                In RSCH   no illusions; only truths   mani-
                fest

                             am I   illusion   or
                             truth

      The passage is so skinny I must enter sideways, adjusting my dead third arm and flapping stomach so they do not obstruct my path. I squeeze in behind Reya, using my unoccupied hand to flatten my front. There is ample space already, but I cannot see it.

Reya maneuvers without issue, turning their crutch-ends to tripods as they move sideways through the narrow crack. They pull me with them, my legs a tangle, into a dark space.

The space is empty in its center and full at the corners, packed so high with jumbled indeterminates that they all meld into one frightening mass. Upon closer inspection, I realize they are not walls at all, but piles of boxes, concealing what—if anything—protects their unseen sides. The darkness is dark such that I am aware I should see nothing, yet the nothing is illuminated so that I know it is nothing and yet see something within. And what was it? Why the boxes, if all could be digitally-stored? Why was the archive archived, and why not yet transcended?

Reya moves toward the boxes, still clicking against the floor with every crutchfall. They pull a box and at first I half-expect the entire mountain to tumble with it. Though the archive trembles, it does not fall. The box comes forward and Reya peers inside as if inspecting a garment drawer.

"It's the hormones. The supply." Reya says. Speechless, they gesture me over.

I jog toward their darkened shape. I have not jogged since before all of this and feel pain in the soles of my feet and a strange shifting in my guts and my chest as if something of me shakes free in every bound. Perhaps this is how I will lose my arm, my stomach. As I near Reya's shadow-drawn figure, I see the hormones stacked and bathing in their own light. In clear bottles, they lay side by side. Next to the bottles, several clean syringes. The bottles' symbols, which had been obscured in the wild, were clearly marked as "M" or "F," and it was so clear and simple I almost laughed at its painful simplicity.

"I thought you were looking for your legs," I said.

My breath is thick and panting. Panting, like an animal, long since forbidden by RSCH authorities as dirty, body-chained beasts. Only the deviant were like animals, and that is why they   we   live in the dirt and the trees. What am I, if not chained to the body that brought me here? I stare down at the clear bottles which had remade me.

"I *am* looking for them," says Reya, picking up an "F" marked bottle and putting it down again. They reach sideways into another box and return triumphant with a needle and injector. They halve their crutches, sinking to the floor as their legs contract. Thigh-length from the floor, they rest their quartered crutches on the ground, arms held parallel and thighs angled as if kneeling.

They look at me expectantly, syringe in an outstretched hand, eyes gesturing at the open box now above them.

Hand shaking, I reach into the box, hold an "F"-marked bottle up in a question mark.

"I doubt anyone can open this," I say.

"Just try. Just try, being no one. That's the thing, right?"

I sigh. Not this again.

"I'll always have been someone."

"No. Just try,   . See, where did your name go? No one. It just happened into the air and became nothing at all."

I stick the bottle into my nobody mouth and bit the top. It acquiesces. The substance tastes like poison. I do not know what poison tastes like but when I taste it I read poison inside, and the surge of text alone near-knocks me off my feet. More rivulets leak into my mouth from the lid now between my teeth. Coughing, I drop the thing while keeping the fluid inside.

Then I press my mouth to Reya's. I open my lips. I feel Reya's tongue and let them scrape the liquid from my teeth.

Reya pulls my face closer, holding my head against theirs with a steady hand against my neck. Then, they push me away in order to pull their garment, which had pooled on the ground around them, up around their waist.

I reach for another bottle marked "F". This one I open with my mouth, but more gently than the last. I fill the syringe and press the needle into Reya, closing my eyes as it enters their skin. Behind my lids I see the greenspace, I see a walking gang of deviants all in a line.

> Illicit organizations of deviants/ deviance bent on sowing disharmony, known for physiological and psychological uncleanliness.

We had stopped walking in this way when **RSCH** started **hiring**, hormone shortages worsened exponentially, our sporadic supply dwindled to none. They were here. Consigned to past as if a   basement. On the other side of these boxes, if the wall—if a wall—is the green I begin now to recall. They make the deviants here. Just outside the house of light.

Once, RSCH had sat us in a group, deviants preparing together to Recitizen. We were fuzzy outlines to each other, visible as a group only to the faceless moderator, who sat on a semi-raised platform at the head of the circle. Heorshe talked down to us and we listened with upturned faces and wide eyes. Heorshe looked like heorshe was being cut into pieces by small tunnels, which did not enter hisorher body but faded into the vague, surrounding halo. We were to imagine ourselves likewise connected, likewise enflowed.

We took the shake together, myself included. It was a conduit to something. I carried it with me like a block in the pit of my stomach. It leaked out of each pore like its own sick halo.

I reach for another bottle, but recoil instantly. This drawer contains no hormones, but instead a severed arm, metal and golden-brown with what I recognize as *rust*, an ancient affliction whose beauty—was this beauty?—at this moment, stunned me. I open the drawer directly above to find several fingers made of Uncitizen skin. Now the skin was RSCH, as it always had been. I thought about Reya's legs, no longer theirs. No longer there. Other things I was accustomed to seeing severed. Except, they were not severed, because RSCH was Pure, RSCH was whole. RSCH was and was not the cut fingers.

I had felt so adrift, a cut limb myself, staring up at the blurred mediator and hisorher pulsating halo as if I were not yet worthy, as if my eyes were not yet capable. Together we spoke about the reasons we were axed. We would learn how to be good so we did not cause a future axing. We learned the reasons we were to commit   to rescuing   axing   others in return for our time here. **Here is what you did to end up here, and here is how we will help you get better.** RSCH, generous. RSCH, kind. RSCH, forgiving of the missteps that led to us leading to them leading making us unmake.We learned gratitude. We **could have been expelled for good. But someone, somewhere, believed in our capacity to get well**—believed that there was a well Citizen waiting inside me, desperate to fulfill her duty.

I did not believe it and yet I did; my mind was a track running in dizzy circles.

Reya attacks high-up drawer with their crutch, now fully-extended. They lean against the lower drawers for support, opposite crutch a counterbalance. Soon a rectangular thing with rounded corners falls from somewhere above. They pick it up, then drop it at once.

"Is this made of *paper*?" They asked me, shoving a sheet into my hands, but grimaced as if they knew the answer. They ran a hand over it again. They may have continued with this if the paper did not draw their blood, a thin crescent on their forefinger. This time, they did recoil, and their blood dotted one rounded corner.

I took the bloody thing. It was not paper; when I pressed it, it turned red, before slowly fading back to starch-white. It could have been a body part. In a certain light, it could have   been a text. Perhaps it is a test. The words are, perhaps, made of holes. It gestures at the body of its sourcing.

"It looks a little like an arm, don't you think?" asks Reya. "Or a tiny leg. Too tiny, unless—" Reya closes their eyes. We recall the little boy. We let him go together with grudging pity.

I continue to examine the thing. "Look at this, like a vein," I say. "It has to be an arm, you can tell. It's just all flattened out. That's where the wrist would be." I point to a vein-raised mound slightly warmer and redder than the rest.

The longer I squint at this text, the more it seems like an arm; the more its words appear not ink but blood. I see other mounds, not veins but fingers squeezed together until one.

&each finger, a line.

&each line, a sentence.

I hold a record.

I blink once. In the blink I see, just for a moment, a document alone. Then, it becomes an arm once more, growing denser until it is too heavy to carry.

Reya moves to other drawers, not opening them with abandon and allowing their contents to clatter to the floor. No more have hormones. Instead, they contain grotesque gestures at bodies long gone, bodies whose rest rests, no doubt, in the forest, where everything was forbidden.

Reya reaches into another drawer, dragging one finger across the not-paper inside. They lick residue the color of blood from their fingertip. The text they lift is swollen and discolored beyond recognition. I have no idea what limb or appendage it was meant to be, if any; it could as easily have been a grotesque hybrid of several bodies stuck to one another, a true affront to RSCH (in whose belly we defect). The text was a body, once, just like all the rest, but its mottled shades of red and brown contrast sharply with the inside of the drawer's blue innards.

Reya turns the thing in their hands. "This is mine, I'd say." They look then to their thighs, holding the thing between their stumps and the floor as if trying it on.

"What are the chances of that?" I ask.

They continue to turn it. I strain to catch their eyes, eyebrows, piece of a nose and flash of a lip from its corners.

"I'm taking this out," they say, not answering. "It's mine now. Who knows if I'll find...mine. If they ever were mine. So I claim this."

"And how do you think we're going to do that? Get out, I mean? And with that thing?"

Again I hear the voices that we heard on our descent. They spoke as if advising, but not loudly enough to hear.

"It's me now. It's my body, so be nice." said Reya. "I claim it. Whatever is written here." I could now discern some illegible text on the thing, too damaged to read.

Reya places their leg below their stumps. We pull another box. This time, we find ears, pale white and exquisite, as if carved by hand. Reya holds them to their ear and listens. I listen to the voices in the walls. No, not the walls, the boxes. The words inside.

"I can hear something," said Reya. "And... I say these are mine, too." So they were. Nothing was Reya's. These were nothing—abandoned pieces from unbodied bodies, the underside of RSCH. I sit inside that logic for a moment, pleased with my Imagination. I didn't think it would work here. I didn't unthink it, either.

●

The air is clear down here. The light trickles in from outside green. The wild light an irony piercing RSCH darkness. It is cold, but not as dry as in the halls or rooms. For all of RSCH's fears of the dark, this blackness surrounding us is clean and smooth; in the shadows I feel unbodied just as RSCH desires. This clarity means I live right up against my fear until I cannot feel it anymore, until I am so intimate with it that I forget there are other parts of me.

Shadows well could live

me up against my fear until a point

less thing to feel.

Right now, any number of drs could be observing my limp and hollow side, my second stomach and defunct third arm. I could still be in my room. This could be my test. This could be the axe again, another act, a summoning. This could be a staging ground, just before time starts.

Yet there is also power in this basement, just like in the forest: all these abandoned pieces so noxious they have nothing   left to lose. Like them I am only left over, body in excess of its usable data, in excess of its feeling, far past time.

> Time does not pass if RSCH does not record it to be so, because RSCH and RSCH alone is fully aware of the mechanisms of time-tracking and documentation, and time-tracking is accessorized by contemporaneous data, which is considered to be such when matching RSCH timestamps.

Reya rummages for more legs. They are amassing a collection, now up to at least sixteen pairs. Each appears both leg and document, some bloody, some not; some white and some brown and some black, all bone and muscle and flesh fat hanging gelatinous in a great frozen dribble.

"I keep thinking about how close we are," says Reya. "Walking here, all this time."

We looked to the still-shining green, light almost menacing against the cool shadow.

"We're on the other side now, but in some ways, we're already back there. Or, we never left. *There* was here all along,   ."

My name still blurs in their mouth. I feel something like safe in the nameless; as if I am the absence in which we stand. As if the blank absence is my name now. My name a door, a key, a hole, a mark, a window, a carving.

I remember shapeless-traipse the green outside until eyes ache understare. Boxes, cartons. Eyes dry enough to crumple at next blink. More of me back like waves. Move　　　　　　of me back like clatterboxes. Voices chatter round and I am closer. I am branches into roots. I am

Is there such a thing
as a wild space,
if RSCH is the one
that makes it? If RSCH is
That which names—

Is there such a thing
as freedom if it's to RSCH
to write the word—

if RSCH makes Uncitizens
what is to be done
what is   un

14. Nothing was so different

I grew up just normal enough to skate, just *ab*normal enough always to be on the lookout. Nothing was so different about me when I started school, but each day I'd arrive home with a tingling urge called "seek." I tried to unthink seek, but it came back the more I **STOPped** it. I needed more. I was hungry in the Impure way.

Before, I didn't know Reya. They weren't around. They weren't even Reya.

My life went on like this. Like all parents, mine left in the early morning to arrange data. I went to school, performed my coursework and supplemental socialization training. I returned home in the mid afternoon to complete my monitored independent work using attention-tracking tech. Each day, hours later, my parents would return. In the evening we would drink the shake together and then retire to our beds.

I learned to eagerly anticipate the coming of meals, to traipse into dedicated spaces and feel *something*, even if that something was disgust and violation. I learned to hate myself for the anticipation. I learned to hide my hatred into compliance.

Even if I worked twice as hard to **STOP** the sensations I felt when the shake hit my tongue, so as not to be presented with the slice, or worse.

Then, Reya entered. I don't know how they got in, what they presented to the teachers and administrators to get themself approved. They were simultaneously there and not-there, never called by name yet visible to us and to our educators; beholden to the rules of the school yet in violation by virtue of their own existence. It hurt my head to think about, but I was drawn to them. Drawn in ways I struggled to understand. Some ways simply hurt the bridge of my nose and others caused a faint rising deep beneath my stomach. Reya caused me many sensations, all of them deviant.

They led me to wonder to the edges of my wondering. Why couldn't I think outside this space before being told that something else was there? Why did I, this whole time, feel so far outside of my body? What stopped me, and only me, from wrangling the meat into a submissive posture, riding my mind on the back of the thing and catapulting from the body to the better? Why? What defects have manifested, how can they be purged? How was I a Citizen if I harbored these inherent impurities?

I entered adolescence.

I entered the wilds.

I began the hormone regulators. Hair grew on my chest and chin. My voice deepened. I had only the river as mirror but I knew I did not look like her.

In the immediate wake of the shake and my mother and the recordings, I went to school as if nothing were amiss, **STOPping** my thoughts and protecting against perseveration. I would walk through the front doors, through the body scanner, receive the instant weight and vital sign check required of me that would then be sent to all teachers and other educators. EyeScan ensured I was in the building, made a small satisfactory sound and sent a file somewhere. I proceeded as normal through my classes and lunch and learned comportment with all the others.

Some things had changed, though. It was like an intake of another kind, its own little axe. I was no longer allowed to walk on my own from classroom to hall to dining space. I was carried on a long and narrow stretcher, wrists and ankles held by distancing devices so that educators could hold me without touching. The metal was hard and cold. My skin remembered its private contortions. At lunch I would sit between two supervisors at the long, narrow table, those with highest compliance sitting toward the outer edges, those who required disciplining near the gut of the thing, right where its two halves connected with a hinge at which the tables could be folded at will. Right between the supervisors, I sat at the hinge. I felt it beneath my garment. My mother could watch the meal through the contacts, of course, but normally she did not have time amid her data-sets.

The dining room was an open space, without shadow or crevice. It had several tall windows from which light shone in. Each of us sat in a high-backed chair and squinted against the brightness.

There were no clocks in the dining room. Against the sun there was no way to read them. We were expected to intuit the time—more than intuit, *know*—because RSCH was the correct time, RSCH *had* the correct time—knew it, because it was Truth, and because they knew it   was   to be true. We drank in time with one another. Our faces would be scanned periodically, at intervals unbeknownst to us, throughout the meal, attempting to detect a disturbed emotional state.

> I ask, I asked, why is it always the shakes: why consumption. Because all life is a thing to consume
> or to expel, all RSCH is to eat up or reject. All rules, swallowed
> to the body, and we were started young. Consume, con
> -tract, what will   ing

to take inside?

Reya would drink in time with us. They told me later that they didn't mind, that the shake tasted wrong but it was good to be in company. They found it strange, though, the collective commitment to *watching*—our eyes felt like little gears in one great seeing machine, and our heads swiveled automatically from diner to diner. Reya compared it all to breathing—not just the drinking shakes, but the classes, the work, all the consumption. It all felt too closed to them; especially as an outsider whose outsider status was a fatal secret. They compared the system to the Community itself, closed yet forced, in its closure, to acknowledge its fear of the elsewhere.

"How's that?" I had asked them. That day, they were trying to take my mind off the feelings the shake gave me, feelings that made me feel like I was RSCH sent to axe myself, yet stymied at every turn because the axe-wielding thing was precisely that which I, the wielder, needed so badly to destroy.

"I've had a lot of time to think. And I've watched. Seeing is breathing, you know?"

"That's nonsense," I said. Several forms of deviance were in part characterized by engagement with and propagation of *nonsense*, expressly different from *dissension*, a symptom unto itself.

"All right, report me, then. Have them check the database for my name. See if they can call me *Reya*. See what happens if they try to see me. Try to count someone they're not allowed to say exists."

Like breathing, seeing was: involuntary, compulsory, restricted, monitored. The contacts inundated us with a constant stream of messaging, impossible to turn off, even while sleeping. During the day it was mostly the Network. At night, brain-training as we slept. What we saw around us, the contacts saw: they both augmented reality and re turned it to RSCH.

Reya told me early on that they did not have the contacts, and this was in part the reason they could move without detection. I felt a wiggling resentment toward them for that and for many things. Later, they would admit they resented me, too, for having the luxury of choosing my own defection.

On the surface, a body bloats
grows wide with nothing
bleeds an absent excess.
I am told the shake
will help me concentrate.
I am told I am inadequate
and sink
into inadequate as though I know
and I know
it was a word
made for me

like blood, unsure
how to pump unturgid
like temperature cannot take itself
like
there is a time
the body, so tired it ceases
to tire at all,
shapes into a spoken wheel
stomach hand head foot
stumble in their lineward likeness
linewords making what
of body can be said
while still evading
the digestive tract

None of it *felt* chosen. I had escaped to the woods in the night in a half-sleeping state, just before my body was set to wake. I could hardly walk straight or open my eyes but stumbled past the houses and the fences, dragging myself across the endless buffer between the Community and the wilds, ripping the skin from my chest, stomach, and thighs as I crawled over the sharp barrier substance and into the illegible beyond.

And then, the Operator, to consecrate my tears.

"I want a chunk of my side—I don't care what side—cut out and I want you to suspend in the empty space an expandable bag made of some strong material to collect those things I ingest   in jest   and can be cleaned and emptied at will."

This is what I told the Operator when I asked, no, begged for the stomach. It looked at me with its normally-blank hand-eyes and I swore I saw some expression in them, a doubt probably native to my own mind. Another distortion, just one of a litany.

It had hesitated before replying to me. It had never performed such a procedure before. Reya told me later that the face I made while asking concerned them, too. I looked to those eye-hands hands with such brutal desperation.

And I was desperate in ways Reya would never understand. They didn't know what it meant to have grown up consuming, only consuming, the material that would make a RSCH out of me, too—merging with a Community, one data set and another and into thousands of meaningless, meaning-rich sentences to build disparate walls and barriers and shackle me to their insides. They did not understand the panic. They did not know what it felt to destroy this great network of skin and fat and bone that truthed perpendicular to RSCH. They had only bad memories and the hurt of my screams.

Anyway, the night of the stomach. The woods were dark on the night of the stomach. I could have died.

I didn't die. I spent the next several days hazy and listless, and the Operator came to visit me frequently, eyeing its hands into the wounds it had caused. I remember feeling its hand-eyes so tender and shocked, though they did nothing but see and sew. They blinked something like care into my wounds. I recall the feeling of its lashes dancing against the great, gaping whole, hole in my side giving way to a suspended stomach-bag connected to the rest of me by tubes. It was all reds and grotesque yellow-browns, with several small spots of green.

In the beginning, I could hardly wiggle my fingers, never mind lift an arm or walk. The pain of becoming lingered inside, first sharp, then dull and aching. I felt like I was pulling myself along by a trail of heavy memories whose tie to I couldn't break—no longer in possession of a stomach, I now had its phantom. Half of my abdomen, the nameless organs inside of it and surrounding tissue, were no doubt buried with the rest of the bodies deep in the woods, as was I.

I began wrapping myself in moss every night. It felt like something resembling the safety, that quality RSCH mandated. Safety was cover, provision, soft expectation—moss was all of those things, even when I struggled to fall asleep. Over time, I squinted the Community into focus less often. I tried to live without reference to it. I tried to think beyond the before that made me. I forgot what it was to feel rest, another quality whose attainment was mandatory and monitored in the Community.

> Every day, waking, walking to school, led in lines from room to room and lesson to lesson, returning home to work till dusk in a bleached white room. My mother and father came home at dusk, and we would eat. After that came the rest-period which bled into night. We would get clean and retreat to our rooms, at whose clicking locks we would begin a strange hypnosis, relent to sleep. In the morning, the same sound woke us and beckoned us back to school and work and ritual. Its quiet constriction was not truly detectable while I was in it.

I scaled back my consumption. I did not Imagine a world without RSCH. I turned away from a life of safety, which was really just a life of tender fear.

●

Below my memory, a layer of text. Marked as me. I watch the earlier-woman I saw could have been myself marking it. She betrayed no sign of my knowing. I see her head, her knows, her skin, her woman uniform wrapped round her body, round and long as a gesture. I saw her from the ceiling and knew she was whole. She remained a Citizen   of integrity.

As she marked the page, as she caught the data, I marked the flesh. As if the basement itself was grow-ing the stuff, as if our bodies were mere symptoms of RSCH, as if it grew us   appendages

I scratched and the walls shouted back at the woman I watched look above herself as if attempting to find   attempting to find me, am I a vowel, am I disrupting, am I a disruptive space

I angle nearer to her shoulder. I try to fly closer down but some field stops me. From where I hover I see no specific words so I imagine them, replete with the gaps that

REPORT: SUBJECT RE-VISION [contaminated ver.]

100   /
PRODUCT #429082
COL: ULTM

A dose of   per   will 1) siphon bodily pollut-
ants, including extraneous

(RSCH cannot pollute and thus foreign substances administered by them are not foreign but natural although it is only un-naturality that compels RSCH to administer such substances to Impure bodies whose impurity is to be solved by the ad ministra-tion of foreign substances
so as to make the body
natural, that is, clean of pollut-ants)

chemicals and small unauthorized, implanted devices 2) opti-mize memory for integration and Recitizenship 3) to render open storage space to as to study, engage further with architec-ture of defective body/mind.

Administered intravenously by   per   . un-less otherwise directed; hue, viscosity; duration to vary [see attached] depending on chemical balance; hormonal value

draw   the story   my hair   my body   slack

refuse   forever a child   its hungry   years

spent, yearning   for   the end   a name   any

thing   if   searched, for

Axe 1: Above

Rise   the tawny light. Woods high around us. Bones below. Trees scrape the lid. The real lid, through which the sun. Burns. I see a body in the distance. I am running and so are they. We know this. All know this. The hills we are each running down are the same hill, but we are running each opposite to one another, and this all goes smoothly.

I know it's in my hands. Big bladed. I know the sound my voice made when I begged for a chance. I begged to be the woman I could not be believed in her my only hope   knowing elsewhere underneath.

This was the woman meant to be me and this is where I am and the axe   I am her and I am practicing. I swing at the air. Light chafes our surroundings.

I run, watch as a younger and smaller and more poisonous me makes to swing. I see neither deviant nor person, but instead an axe-wielding cloud of data, every sentence lain as if in accusation. Then, she transforms, and I become a body of severed limbs, their foot-trodden filth, I am every organ I have ever stepped upon. Then, I am her, I am the axer itself.

I know this is data from my own mind. Data mined   b   y RSCH, now seized upon by a hand I cannot see. I am watching what might be possible. Sentences. My sentence. The cat drinks milk. My window is broken. The store is closed. Again, a wiggling foot. A thigh. Several eyes, lolling at random beneath the axe-blade. Fragments. Amalgamations of all I have already seen. I pull back, let go. The scene dims. I do not float toward the poisonous me. This me did not swing. The pile lolled, spat, made unnatural sounds, sounds I anticipated would continue long after I left. If there was leaving.

Axe 2: Rage Forest

This is the rage forest   suck

tight

       My stomach pumped of vital toxicants before I let myself loose
on who   se   ever misfortune it was today to cross my
path, plagued by memories—false—of my own indulgence and
casting my childself upon the poor unsuspecting victim who will
meet my blade which is not my blade but appears to be held by
my arm, not my arm, but a rschRSCH RS   chCH   patent
arm that is marked ascribed to me

swing   MAYBE IF I KILL HER I WILL FORGET HER NAME
blunt

WHEN I FORGET HER NAME
glut
             whip   the axeblade
swing   WHEN

      WHEN I FORGET HER NAME I WILL TURN   HER
      STOMACH
      TO A HOLE THROUGH WHICH I   STEP
      AND TURN AWAY
clutch   FROM TRUTHS THAT DO NOT FIT INSIDE
      MY MOUTH   whip
             whip   PILE

BAD PILE
MY PILE MY BAD   MY GREAT
MY PILE MY OH MY   MY GROTESQUE   MY

Anything if searched for. So I find a crack. I must work
it open. I decided it would be a membrane. I watch the wall. I dare it with
my eyes. I continue to see the beckoning green.

"We were so close," says Reya again. "All that time. It's so green."

"We knew it then. Where else could the hormones have come from?
We saw the walls. We knew we were alive, even if we weren't."

The climate outside the wild is unsuitable for life. While the wild is
contaminated, RSCH Knows it, whereas the outside is nothing at all.

"We chose not to," they say. "I chose not to, and that's how I
stayed…" They didn't say alive. They didn't say   didn't   stay
safe.

I think about the crack I plan to make, a slice between the green,
a barely-visible fold. I don't think it too hard for fear of giving it up, but I
underthink it when I am not looking. Always, the underthinking. Thinking
not like roots but the holes they leaf. I dig a hole in myself and set up there,
wondering when we might catch up to each other.

I close my eyes and listen to the voices in the walls speak their data.
I take what I could for public record, siphoning, siphoning. I try to hear my
own.

Axe 3: EX_PULSE

We were tougher again. I mean, together   again.   We walked through the forest. Neither of us had an axe. I did not want to kill any part of myself. I did not want to kill the things Reya made me notice about myself. They carried legs beneath their arms. My own extra arm beneath the arms worked again, had overcome its atrophy.

I tried to tell Reya of the legs, "Don't, they'll take them back." I ask them if they remember what they said about their body, about the little capsule. Surely, one of these things: this walk or the memory, must be a dream. But which? When I opened my mouth to ask my words turned liquid and I vomited a thick blue sludge. I felt better but not in the cruel way. Reya moved from my side and toward an overwhelming tree. They offered me their crutches to hold after lowering themself onto the soil, stubs against earth.

There was a process called **_mourning_**—or was it **_grieving_**?— that **they performed in the past**. I have mentioned this before but feel it bears repeating for the public record if there is to be a remainder between my body and the text.

(Although what of this becomes the public record will indeed only be the remainder after the Truth is done with them)

Again: **Grieving is a process that appeared intricate with its multiple steps. Instead of being quarantined and treated, you malingered in it and others watched, even partook.**[9] Now the dead were the dead and the disappeared the disappeared, the rejected consigned to the forest that did and did not exist. Reya buried their legs beside us, digging a suitable, shallow hole with their fingernails. Dirt crusted and grumbled beneath them. When they were done, they sucked the dirt from their

---

9 Grief is always past tense.

fingernails and spat it in the place their legs had lain. They added extra spit
and rubbed it all around with the base of their crutches.

I do not anticipate the axe this time. It flies into my hand so unnat-
urally, as if an afterthought. I wonder what preceded it. I wonder if I could
have **STOPPED** it, where it would have gone. I wonder what I could be
if I were no longer a conduit for the killing   RSCH couldn't
be. I wonder if I was no longer tucked into that which killed me until it had
sucked each and every ounce

I asked Reya if, now that their legs were in the hole and all the bodies
surrounded them, they felt a little closer to transcendence. **This**, it was said,
was the goal. Transcendence. To leave the body. Reya left their
body in the hole and so I said, "Reya, you are the first deviant to transcend,"
and they said, "I don't need to transcend because I don't exist. How's that,
RSCH?"

They screamed it. I heard it as a scream and told them so. "HOW'S
THAT, RSCH?" They laughed, whispering, "if they say they hear me it
means they're hearing something unreal and how bad for them would that
be? Ruined!"

They leaned in and pressed their lips to mind   mine.   Hard.
They reached around my waist. The rest is an understory but we know it
already.

I need a plan, but not my own plan, because RSCH planned and any plan planned by me would be theirs, or so I feared, because   did so much blue now make me   more   RSCH   than I? And how to unplan? Even in my hacking days, I followed a meticulous course. I brought order to the wild in a way Reya sometimes mocked, or, when I whittled myself into a neat row of ribs and little else, feared.

I begin to say, "we need to try something thoughtless," and as I do Reya walks from their place beside the limbs to a far wall. Blue cascades down its face, glowing. To my horror, Reya dips a thumb into it.

"You just messed that up. Just *do*. Don't talk anymore." Their hand hands beside my face. I sense the blue. It casts a cold shadow.

"Don't even think words."

"Speak for yourself."

I lick, pointedly anticipated nothing. I close my eyes until I see blue inside the lids. I open them, see mid-darkness and Reya and deep, deep color dripping from their thumb to the floor.

They try to say my name. "   can you hear me?"

"I... I don't know what you tried to call me. But I'm still here." I take another suck of their thumb. It tastes only of salt. It is saltwater. I suck again. Reya sighs.

What had I expected of the blue? Formally, nothing; inside, perhaps, a revelation. Or an erasure. But nothing happened. Time did not slow or start or speed. I was not thrust into another displaced memory. I take a hesitant lick. Still salt.

"It's nothing," I say. "It doesn't trigger anything. I feel the same." No particular past events overtake my consciousness. My memories, such as they are, feel firm. I remember the blue color against the white white room, the jolts of otherselves each blueing tube brought. But the blue does not remember me. I mine my mind and nothing askew.

Reya licks some themself. They are not overtaken, either, although their memory has only ever faced the power of the chip.

"Does this mean I had something in me all along? A chip?" I ask Reya, before I can stop myself. What caused all this, if the blue was—if RSCH could lie, which they could not   and yet   —a cover, a ruse?

Reya spins me around and paws at my neck and upper-back. There is nothing. I already knew there was nothing. They say, "No scar. No trace."

We return to the body texts, unsure of what else to do. We attempt again to read them. We do not treat the unclaimed pieces with care anymore, only as what they are: the property of RSCH. When I squeeze they empty blood in jagged shapes across my hands and down my wrists and to my arms and still-on gown, thinner than the thinnest of skins. The blue seems to cower in the face of it.

In the corner of my mind I see a figure forming out of all the stolen parts, but this figure collapses or changes as soon as I try to see. Its hair grows and falls, its skin turns mottled and then smooth. From within, it illuminates its litany looks. It is a girl, it is a boy, it is like and unlike Reya, like and unlike me, a girl who wasn't. The creature floats to my shoulder, evades my touch. The figure could be me. A girl, a boy, a something not like Reya but like in difference, a something, a girl   who wasn't, a girl   RSCHd   then discarded, memory kept as evidence of her rejection like stairs to a place more precious

She fomented in an unthought place. I aimed to visit

    the memories like stairs   precarious

    upon the data-boxes   dreaming-dreaming

Reya mops the floor with their garment. They are naked and dripping sweat. Their crutches pull red with each fall.

I remember speaking to the bodies in the forest. I didn't think they would hear, but I did need to hear myself. I needed to do this *for the public record*, I thought each time. To keep track. And that is what I do. The bodies themselves could hold words, memories, and speeches of mine that I myself did not remember giving. My whole life in the forest was an anticipation of my eventual unfreedom, which was itself a form of confinement. Yet, I needed to free my voice into the bodies that remained.

I poured out my words in the hopes they would tangle in the trees. In the era where food was scarce, I spoke as if eating. I spoke until my voice gave out. I spoke in writing, buried the text inside them.

Some days I wished I was dead. Most of the time I didn't, but it always appeared as if I did. Reya would find me fallen asleep across the barely-buried bodies and grimace. I was too light. We discussed disgust. Those were my bodies, I told them. You have none of your own, they said. I would surely be there someday, I reminded. Sleeping beside them was simply practice.

"They're my friends," I had said once with a dizzy head. "This is…" My mad laughter. My dizzy gut. "This is dinner with friends! And I have been starving—" Laugh, wheeze, "—I have truly been starved of it."

In less-lean times, I did not forget about the bodies. I sat with them, whereas before I had stood, swaying in the timed breeze whose time was not my own.

I continued to speak to the bodies, said things that all made nonsense, all in the shadow of the impossible wall of impossible height and impossible width. Later, from even further afield, I would return beneath the cover of darkness, ready for distribution. The Distributor would hand the Operator the crates of hormones. We'd pass them down the line and take what we could carry. Night would pass into day and I would walk to the stream, cross, see the bodies, look above each of my shoulders and try to make myself at home.

My memory now returns to the carrying. I am aware that I am remembering my body before me. Now I am in my body but I am also the one observing. My body which I am in and observing obeys my commands from below.

But why now, why this time? What happened to the remembering and to the blue that now gives me salt and freedom? Is this, indeed, freedom, or am I giving RSCH a show—an exposure?

(My own paranoiac tendencies still threaten me.

I am RSCH **malingering** itself. I walk a split-truthed path and try to keep the thoughts at bay.)

I wanted to slap myself for using a RSCH word, **malingering**, but I resisted. One side of me is the me in RSCH—no, that is all of me—one side of me remains in the basement, lingering over peoples' pieces, now mere data. The other half is walking here as if I never left. One half reaches into a new crate, and the other, suddenly, notices a facet of their surroundings they did not see before. These events open to time, swallow the remnants, and I am witness.

I return to the dark line we walk. I whisper to my line-mate, stay low, keep quiet. When we think we hear an axe we jump among the bodies and act dead. Dead like the parts below me in their designated crates. Sometimes my feet slip and I step on them by accident. I watch over my shoulder at Reya on the ground below me. I am climbing as if this tower were a tree.

RSCH was impossibly high, I always believed. I still cannot see a top. I see   I saw a vast blackness and I see the parts in front of me. But surely this must end. Surely—

no **CANTTHINKIT**

There is a sky past this enclosure. At least, I must believe there is. I imagine myself piercing through the invisible ceiling only to come up underground. To see no way. But I would not be buried if my emergence were inconsequential. I would not have faced the axe if I was not a credible threat. I must believe there to be a way to do with this life what I did in my dreamline, a place to go back to fiddle in-tense.

Past the wild is an edge. The wild is like dying but it isn't, because though it's forbidden it's also RSCH, RSCH impossibly wide and long and All. At the edge of the wild is the outside, not contaminated but simple Not. Non-space. After anti-life, simply nothing. Where the data might go if RSCH did not collect it, implying the importance of the act of collection. This was the great threat. We learned it in our books. It was so part of us we did not think about it on the surface. We thought about purity, health, sustenance.

Somewhere a woman makes a sentence and it glows satisfactorily blue. She places it among its relevant data points, also sentences. She begins to think about the spaces there between the words. She thinks about grease. She thinks about gaps. She thinks about how many ts and js and entire englishes might be stacked or toppled, the rumbles those falling letters might cause.

Reya calls up to me from their sea of files. They found two ears. Nearby, a nose. Someone is so close I believe I could touch her if she would allow to be touched, and she is someone that I recognize, though also someone I cannot name. Blue drips onto my forehead. I tip my chin up and catch my mouth with several drops, letting them fall one after another, stacking as if letters waiting to be claimed.
Climbed.

    "Hey,   !" I, still nameless, hear Reya's voice from below.

    I look back. I can no longer see them nor the ground, only darkness beneath me. Above, bare light like a life the size of my fingertips. I kept climbing, grasping crates, preparing, soon, to fall. My toes curl mere moments from sets of abandoned limbs. With each step, the thing shakes.

        I wait for more words from Reya. None come. Another tremor shakes the tower and I know it's Reya, pulling another box from below. Still, I do not fall. I feel in some extended way as if they are touching me, snaking their arms through the interladen boxes and gasping round my waist. Feeling held, I discover a stomach in the box above me. It could or could not have been mine. It is mine. It was mine. I held it in my hands as if
I hand   I grasped my hand to   as if to read as if I were   a mouth
    And a light above
    And I took the opening
    as if it were to free

AXE 4: Refuse

when the past is vile
we   remember
we are in the future
we   remember
the history is everything
repeated
many enough times
to linger
to earn   to name   some great
forever

We reached the border between wild and nothing. This time, Reya and I were sitting side by side, as if we were schoolchildren again in that after-space we could ever name.

> (And because we could not
> name it and so it continued
> beneath   the truth un-
> heeded)

We are always together in these nothing spaces because they are in our dreams.

We could make out the glimmer before the border, though it wasn't easy to see. It blended in with the surrounding flora, so densely-packed it nearly obscured the opaque beyond the final branches. If this was all an eye the Community would be the pupil, the wild the unruly iris, and the rest as dense and white as the beyond. Between the iris and the white this glimmering, lace-like ring.

Beyond was only the refusal of place, the result of a history set to destroy itself, as all history does, as all oldworlds made in memory of new.

The coasts sank. Smoke seeped up through tangled tree limbs and Citizens
ran toward the very waters that threatened to swallow them
whole. The terminally-deviant dove from massive, floating structures into an
even larger mass of water, which spread further than my eyes could track.
They fit all the way beneath the waves and did not resurface. And RSCH
watched and governed and made-do and pulled together the brightest of
bright minds to make life, refuse death; make light, refuse the darkness at the
underside of this great hulking title wave threatening to destroy civilization
itself.

Neither I nor Reya believed in anything beyond here. We couldn't;
we couldn't know it. It wasn't like these unlivable wilds, where you could
be as long as you were not a person. No-thing was out there. It was not
the periphery of anything. It was just unthought. Impossible to think inside,
beneath the sun and all that brutal burning heat.

Both of us harbored a quiet desire to go there, into oblivion, the
place where you go when RSCH truths become incompatible with you.
When you are nothing left. But we didn't, because that's where they left the
deviants the first time. Good riddance, we read.

Now we were bad riddance because we were in the wild even
though we do not exist.

Behind us we heard the rustle we know well.

We flee/d to lacy corners. Fearful places overtaken by the dizzy sun.

I could hear Reya calling but they were not calling. I saw the crates
again. We were in the darkness of the basement and at the border of oblivion. In the dream I threw the body at the shimmer. The body. My body. I
through it   at the shimmer and hit metal and felt crates and
bodies crumble beneath me. I staggered, Reya watched from below. I was
climbing. But we were side by side.

There is white above me. The whites turn into houses. The houses
turn to scenes. Each house contains three Citizens. Each house contains
built-in smart devices to collect important data. Each eye containing one
contact. Each lawn precise and dirtless. I felt (once more past) around myself
in the dark basement and lingered at my growing chest hair, thick and thick
and thick like trees or lace itself.

I rest against a low-hanging branch, struggling beneath its own weight. I watch the rows and rows of occupied houses, shapes positiving the spaces between the wild trees.

AXE 5: The Scale

Downward I looked from my place on the wall of boxes and I saw a green path toward Reya like the one the axer ran and ran to me to take me but it was me   the taker   instead. In my other mind's eye (I was always seeing doubly by now) I saw my walking green and mellow by Reya's side, thinking how unusual we were even among the deviants, not solo but always paired, never far from each other, rarely joining loose gangs looking for shared hiding spaces from axers. They made friends this way. They made like Reya and I did, too. They made things they disliked not touching, things that hurt all the more when the axe, as it always did, came down. Living out there, ganged or paired or alone, felt like running on an endless spiral whose downward, deepward movement was slow and inevitable. A thought that would not STOP.

The sky seemed infinite above me. By sky I mean the Community's sky, the lid, this roof, if there were indeed differences between them. If I had not been in here, somehow, all along.

(If I did not Imagine my way out of here I would be climbing forever.)

I acted as if I were reaching for the roof, that I could grasp it if I only stretched enough. I tried not to think in words or plans but images only. I pretended I was about to rise to see the green, even to see an axe with my name on it. I would pick it up and do something, I thought, taking a break from my images. Even if that something were destruction, I would have to break this frozen place that I was in. Otherwise I would stay stuck below, immobile, for good. I kept moving. I trusted that Reya was, too. We couldn't keep redoing the scenes we were given.

Every step upward my feet took left a bent, crumbled, squashed piece behind, things that used to be bodies that were always simply RSCH. As I squashed them I grew   a little clearer. I was not crushing others like myself, I was crushing data, vital data, data that marked the pulse of something much larger than its sum—here, I am almost here. I imagine a ceiling. Present. I am almost at a place where I can reach and touch it. Almost at a place wherein it might manifest.

What is the code for this?

She quickly climbs a tree.

No, no adverbs.

She does violence.

Is that my sentence? Violence? By merely existing I guarantee it. I provoke reprimand. But what kind? I walked across my thoughts with dirty feet. I climbed toward the sky I believed I had to believe could indeed exist. RSCH, too, grew from the bodies beneath it. She scales—*scales, always scales*, I think. She scales the wall. She has reached the top. Prefigure this as if I am recording still. She has been is leaving evidence. Ruin[,] the grammar. I feel parts tumble beneath me, and I think more loudly: RUIN the grammar. R U I N, like RSCH pronounced. So many crates collapse at once I almost lose my footing, but cling to a stray pair of elbows as if they have reached to catch me.

What would be at the top? A mirrored projection of **RSCH is hiring**? Scratched, now, or Pure as ever? Who is to be hired? Where? Where were the drs? Who hires? Who reaches RSCH height?

Somehow I was at the top. The lid was cold and looked like a door. I opened the door because I did not know if I could, but knew with a renewed urgency that I must consider everything possible or impossible and understand it could be happening now.

Is this what the little boy saw? Before Reya?

The door is open but the crawlspace is too small, I thought bitterly. I dragged my long, filthy nails across each opposite arm, hoping for blood. The blood came and dotted my knees.

Forcing myself to consider everything possible and impossible, I squeezed myself into the mouth of the door. I felt the blood drag its trail behind me, felt it soaking into the skin of my toes. I crawled through a worn, cold cavity that opened as if in welcome. The cavity expanded, my blood a willing lubricant.

When I emerged, I was somewhere small and fuzzy and unfocused. It looked like the place you see between sleep and waking, right behind the eyelid. Too short to allow me to stand up straight, but large enough that I could sit comfortably without ducking, the room was tolerably tight. As I blinked, first slowly and then more rapidly, the room shook some of its fuzz, turning a brutal white so bright its corners disappeared. I felt a familiar chill. The fuzziness came back, the former white seemed to have been an illusion.

This was the intake room.

No patience here. When I had come here all that time ago there had been a bed, restraints, and a consistent brutal whiteness that did not give way to fuzz.

Suddenly, the mouth through which I had crawled to the waiting room turned into a window. Below was the familiar green space, dotted by tiny axes. All the usual, sprawling. Axers acting out the violence that both is and is not violence: a not-quite-Citizen has done it, yet its recipients do not exist.

I am also sick of this story.

I'm sick

of the bursts of pain and fear and sadness somewhere so deep it's only data, so deep it's nothing but a stack of sentences on the surface of a page.

I look to the horizon, avoiding the axers below. Blue and green meet somewhere beyond my vision. Hearing static in my ears, I watch the window transform: first shrinking, then clouding, then falling from eye-level to the floor.

I crouch low before the window. I see a Citizen sorting data below. I take my dead third arm as if it were a weapon, ripping it from the few remaining threads of tissue, crusted and blackened, that had once attached it to my side. I bash the the window, unsure of what to do upon its breaking. The Citizen below me looks around, seemingly aware of some disturbance but not of its source. I see her hesitate, move, hesitate again. I imagine myself entering through every wall, seeping like a color.

My spare arm bleeds the bashing. When the blood first hits the window I cannot believe my site: holes form where each successive red hits the window-glass. My fluids are strong. They are tainted. As my blood runs thick and quick, holes join and expand, and glass gives way to empty space. Blood falls, suspending for moments in the air before sizzling, spitting, yellowing and decaying somewhere above the Citizen's head.

Deviant fluids are corrosive to the touch, RSCH warned. In corrosion they do violence—they *are* violence. Without rigorous recovery measures, the Community will relapse into a state of chaos, one drop at a time. And so I am
the weapon.

I am relapse itself. Themselves. Every drop another hole. If I could Imagine it, or imagine outside of Imagining it, I could make myself a hole from here   no   where,   forever

Not a return but an opening. Not a back but keyhole sliver. I could be the little whole. Hole. I could be the seeping through the hole, coming to the Citizen.

15. The Citizen

The Citizen looked a woman. She was frightening.
Familiar.
She had a lot of hair and it was all tied back per RSCH mandate.
She was wearing a standard white garment and white shoes, per RSCH mandate.
The gloves she wore were blue.
(drs gloves were white, their fingers looked like long and flexible teeth)
She sat for an interminable period, surrounded by screens of different shades.
As new sentences flashed, she copied them, transferred data
Increasing exponentially
from place to place. From which to which? Where to who? From place to place,
that's all.
There was no clock. There could have been a clock but to ask for one
to keep track of time
was reassurance-seeking behavior. She knew life
to be divided into quarters, but did not know which
she was in, at present. She knew the sound of the buzzer.
She knew the sound of her shoes in the hall. She knew
the time would sound when the work that day was done. She would go home
and train her brain agile, compare scores to her peers' on the Network.
She would drink the shake and she would sleep and she would wake.
The sound in the wall was   could not be there if RSCH did not say it
so.
No blood was shed in the data-sorting center. Data is clean.
Tomorrow would rise and return to work and again tap the stories in an
english she could see but never speak.
Each sentence, an act   a tiny conquest.

●

I stick my fingers through the hole I bled through. The Citizen suddenly rises and then disappears. I doze as I await her return, wonder after Reya.

When she comes back, she wears an expression of concern normally subjected to monitoring and rigorous questioning by RSCH. She glances around her office. A small note appears on her primary screen. I can not read it, but presume it is an inappropriate-affect warning. She takes a seat and practices deep breaths. She continues her work. If she detects now me, she feigns ignorance. When the day's-end buzzer sounds, she opens the door and steps into the hallway, briefly disappearing from my view.

What was the last sentence she read before she left? The family is ready for bed. No, that one was earlier, perhaps a different day. The rain waters the grass.

Suddenly the window shifts. I can see her in the hall. She walks slowly to its very end, turning right through an invisible door. I follow parallel above, half-expecting to see a dr on the other side, ready to punish her

me for my wandering   mind.

Inside was no dr. No nothing. I can see the emptiness. The room, I realize, is identical to those Reya and I had entered into on our way to the basement. Yet this woman sorts data; she is not a RSCH. She should not be entering, and yet, she does—she does this unimaginable thing that takes my breath away. (I tunnel my thoughts: If she was, she was a RSCH without a name.)

The window below me seems to change location alongside her. I see her back in the long hallway now, a ghost at her side. Before reaching the end, this time, she turns into another empty room. It contains only two doors, the one through which she entered and one, small and shut before her. and I could see her in the long hallway now. She walks toward the opposing door, opens it, and enters a familiar darkness. I know this place, or unknow it. I push my memory to the front of me, blinking to rid the fog.

She descends a steep staircase, nearly vanishing from sight. She coasts the darkness like a reflection. Then, she pauses, and I am caught up, and it is as if I am directly above her again.

Now I am in the basement. All is dark but for that fingerprint of light. She has entered through the back way, and now she is walking straight ahead into the black.

She walks and the light follows. I remember the woods, and I remember Reya, but it is not the all-encompassing sort of memory, it isn't blue, it's possible. We continue to push the darkness back. At the edges of my hearing, an axe falls, but we continue. We pass, again, the stacks and crates. When she arrives at one, she pulls it, glances over each shoulder. I do not see what she does next.

Another axe: a swift slash, a scream, the unbearable silent wake. Feet pleat the ground as the patient is collected, turned in that moment to passive voice. The Citizen looks disoriented, and once more glances over each shoulder. She tenses. I recognize panic. I wonder where her contacts are, how she could be panicking without RSCH intervention.

She carries the pilfered box beside her. She stumbles over a stray pile I recognize as the mess Reya and I left. Reya, the hormones, and the limbs are gone.

The Citizen passes the boxes, walking until she reaches an empty space. It glows green beneath the finger-light. She opens the box. Some blood spills out. Only a Citizen, a data-sorter, she should not be here. She should be incapable of entering the belly. Yet she opens it herself as if inside a vent above a world the size of that container.

She leaves the bloody box for a moment, returns with another. She does the same to this box, allowing the blood to lick her hands and then her tongue to lick the blood. Again, she glanced over each shoulder. Again, a faint green light spills from an invisible place.

Once more, she exists   exist   exits to retrieve a box. She returns and draws blood. Then, she looks upward, not at me but at the thumbprint light. She looks desperate. I make the same face, hoping it will reach her.

Inside each box resides a shapeless text. She pulls each from its container, one by one, and lays them on the floor before her. They are written in an english I cannot read. From each box, then, she retrieves more, more items than could possibly fit inside: gadgets, partial-limbs all made of metal, vials of ambiguous liquid that looked to be neither hormone nor blue. She pulled some I did not recognized. She pulled a microscopic something that I recognized immediately as a contact dressed in black ink.

She returns to the text, shuffling through the pages as she mouths the english I don't understand. When finished, she taps them all into a pile, situates them directly beneath the fingerprint light. She suddenly begins to tear the pages, tears springing from her eyes like violets, and she moves in great weeping heaves that stir the air. When she cannot rip a page with her hands, she uses teeth. When a page cannot be halved or quartered, she renders it jagged. As she renders the pages another   renders. The green, more clearly now, though I still cannot claim to know its existence. We know nothing.

Covered in blood and tears, she stares at the green beyond. The green stares back. She holds the pages to her chest. She murmurs several words, leaves twice the space in silence. To swallow is to something like a burial. She swallows the pages whole so that they kneel at the foot of her stomach. She drinks the blood.

She gulps
soils
makes
possible

Acknowledgements

While reading, I'll sometimes come to a point where I need to mix things up a little. The most convenient way is to flip back to the acknowledgements section, or the notes, or some other non-urgent back matter. I don't know if you also do this, but if so: hi! I'm not going to spoil anything. I hope this message finds you well, or at least, unwell in an interesting way. This is a series of thank-you's.

•

Place: the majority of this book was written on Nipmuc land, colonially known as the u.s. states of "connecticut" and "massachusetts." Subjected to continuous genocide and epistemicide and subject to this day to federal erasure, the Nipmuc are, as of this writing, the only state-recognized tribe in so-called massachusetts. They are the rightful stewards of the land I call my "home."

To whom do you owe your home? How can you make good on the (un) easy kinship you now share? If you are from where I am from, you can start by giving to Project Mishoon, their ongoing archaeological project: https://projectmishoon.homestead.com/Index.html or buying their merch, created by independent Nipmuc artists, at https://www.bonfire.com/store/ hassanamisco-nipmuc-nation-tribal-merch/.

Origins: The germ that would become this book sprouted in response to a call for submissions from the since-defunct *Mad Scientist Journal*. A seventeen-year-old college freshman who had until then published only in a few e-zines and their high school literary journal, I was looking to do something with my writing that I had not done before. That something, as it turns out, was (in part) "getting paid," which MSJ did upon publishing my short story, titled *Failure to Comply*. This experience—of submitting my first-ever story, getting accepted, and getting paid and sent a print copy of the issue I was in—was an invitation into the universe I now occupy. I could not have asked for a better one. Thank you to MSJ co-editors Dawn Vogel and Jeremy Zimmerman for your patience, grace, and trust. I would not have this book without you.

People: Andrea Lawlor's Advanced Projects seminar, taken during my senior undergraduate year at Mount Holyoke College, whipped this draft, tenderly, into something resembling "completeness." Thank you, Andrea, for the generosity with which you approach, well, everything. And, in particular, for telling me about *Dhalgren*.

I'm a very lucky debut novelist. Jason Sommer's—and, as such, featherproof's—enthusiasm, editorial expertise, and camaraderie have made the scariness of The Debut a little smaller, and a lot more fun. Addie Tsai's publicity genius and joyful friendship have been vital to getting this book from my heart to your hands. Zach Dodson's cover art is fucking awesome.

Creative comrades have sustained me multiply over the eight years since I first dreamed the story of this book. They include, but are, crucially, not limited to (like i, "I" am often forgetful): Samuel Ace, wK blair, tommy wyatt blake, ulysses/constance bougie, KJ Cerankowski, Dorothy Chan, sarah clark, Sarah Dauer, hannah sullivan faknitz, Twoey Gray, Nora Sizhen Hikari, SG Huerta, Naseem Jamnia, Joyce Kung, Sara Lefsyk, Jacquelyne Luce, Mordecai Martin, West Matuszak, Valerie McLaren, Megan Milks, Rita Mookerjee, mix moss, Claire Oshetsky, Briar Ripley Page, Isaac Pickell, Elsie Platzer, Jane Shi, Willa Smart, J. Logan Smilges, Rivers Solomon, MT Vallarta, Iris Xie, &&& everyone at the Remote Access Archive/Liminal Lab.

Let's dream

together
forever

(repeat)

:Okay?

Survival / Postscript:

Thank you to Katherine, for giving me (more) life;
Thank you to Jennie, for hanging together

          , ,

               from the

                       cliffspace

where reason falls.

Thank you to my parents, Beth-Ann Payne and Chris Cavar, who made my life possible (though not always likely). I guess I am the result of your unwavering faith.

To Beth and Chris, and to Delia Hannon, Elliot Cervi, & Gwen McSeveney, for loving me firmly.

Notes

I wrote most of this book convinced I was bullshitting. I had not had very many encounters with writing describable as "experimental" prior to college. My knowledge of "theory" (the kind restricted to academic institutions, anyway) was limited to Judith Butler passages shared on Tumblr. This *undercommoning*, to paraphrase Fred Moten and Stefano Harney, of knowledge created a passageway from the mess of my experience to the architecture of academic discourse, and, eventually, the tools to intervene in it. As reading Tracy K. Smith's *Life on Mars* and Hieu Minh Nguyen's *Not Here* in my dorm room bed helped me to realize the promise of poetry, a concurrent combination of my experiences with institutionally "unaffiliated" digital interlocutors and with my campus-bound comrades have helped me grow into this book.

Critical-creative Black scholarship on fugitivity, opacity, and speculative praxis have (in)formed the ways in which I / i found our way through—and "out" of—this book. Of particular interest are Alexis Pauline Gumbs's *Spill* trilogy, Saidiya Hartman's *Wayward Lives, Beautiful Experiments*, Fred Moten's *Black and Blur*, C. Riley Snorton's *Black on Both Sides: A Racial History of Trans Identity*, Legacy Russell's *Glitch Feminism*, and La Marr Jurelle Bruce's *How To Go Mad Without Losing Your Mind*.

There are few explicit call-backs in this book, but here are two: the reference to "rejectedness" in the Forest is derived from Susan Wendell's early Disability Studies text *The Rejected Body*. The forest itself was conceived, in part, in relation to Eli Clare's vision of the forest as (a) transcrip//ed//spacetime in *Exile and Pride*.

Janelle Monae's entire discography, but primarily their *Archandroid* suite of albums, have been critical to my conception of transMad cyborg-android potentiality, as have transMad readings of Ridley Scott's *Blade Runner* (1984). Early in the writing of this book, I listened to a bootleg audio recording of Donna Haraway's *A Cyborg Manifesto* while walking down an Amsterdam street. It was spring on the Centurbaan's sidewalk and pink petals fell on my feet as I wept.

Lastly, in case it was not already abundantly clear, I was reading a lot of Foucault as I wrote this. A lot. Maybe too much? You be the judge. Just don't be the RSCH.

featherproof BOOKS

Publishing strange and beautiful fiction and nonfiction
and post-, trans-, and inter-genre tragicomedy.

Available at bookstores everywhere,
and direct from Chicago, Illinois at

www.featherproof.com

Printed in the USA
CPSIA information can be obtained
at www.ICGtesting.com
JSHW021921251124
74260JS00005B/97